"*I Will Die in a Foreign Land* chr̲ ̲looked like in 2013 and 2014, as a̲........ties with NATO and the European Union."
RINA TORCHINSKY, NPR

"Sometimes, fiction does a better job of getting to the heart of a subject than nonfiction. This unusual novel takes place during the 2014 Maidan protests that ended in bloodshed and precipitated the removal of Ukraine's pro-Russian president, Viktor Yanukovych. It follows several characters as they participate in the protests and learn to live with unimaginable loss in the midst of violent upheaval and repression."
EILEEN GONZALEZ, *BOOKRIOT*

"This bold, intricate novel is as rich and complex as the Ukrainian history it describes with such precision and longing. In spite of their unspeakable personal and political tragedies, the people in this book will fill you with hope for a better world long after you turn the last page."
MARIA KUZNETSOVA, AUTHOR OF *OKSANA, BEHAVE!* AND *SOMETHING UNBELIEVABLE*

"*I Will Die in a Foreign Land* is of the best kind of protest novels: one that makes you cry, and then makes you mad as hell. It is so far the best artistic treatment of the Euromaidan and Crimean situation, at turns tense, melancholy, and over-abundantly compassionate. This book is both the napalm and the bandages in one."
CONOR HULTMAN, SQUARE BOOKS (OXFORD, MS)

"While expansive, this is an intimate portrait of the human condition, proving that even in the darkness, there is hope."
ADAM VITCAVAGE, *DEBUTIFUL*

"Via a chorus of voices infused with folklore, this novel follows four individuals during a volatile Ukrainian winter, as their lives become intertwined and are forever changed by the protests triggered by their president's alignment with Russia instead of the EU in 2013."
NEW YORK PUBLIC LIBRARY, "A BEST BOOK OF 2021"

"Protests that sparked the 2014 revolution in Ukraine provide the context for Pickhart's dazzling debut novel. Drawing from the folkloric oral history of Ukraine and fusing it with the reporting from journalists, Pickhart focuses on a quartet of characters at the center of a Kyiv protest against the president in which more than 100 people were massacred. Pickhart fully develops these intersecting characters, from an American doctor to a former KGB spy, deftly changing points of view, all of which is enhanced by a chorus of past Ukrainian singers killed by a Russian czar."
THE NATIONAL BOOK REVIEW

"The historical novel *I Will Die in a Foreign Land* is a love letter to Ukraine, its people, and its ability to rise up from piled catastrophes."
FOREWORD

"Pickhart's characters are rich and real, flawed and scared, brave and noble. They betray and they are betrayed, sexually and politically and in every other way. They are shaped by individual choices and the terrible choices forced on them by history. They're humans caught in a current... By telling stories of those who live in history but refuse to fully succumb to it, Pickhart recuperates the humanity of the people of Ukraine and celebrates their lives as human beings, not as footnotes to someone else's history."
BRIAN O'NEILL, *NECESSARY FICTION*

I Will Die in a Foreign Land

a novel by

KALANI PICKHART

Two Dollar Radio
Books too loud to Ignore

Two Dollar Radio

WHO WE ARE TWO DOLLAR RADIO is a family-run outfit dedicated to reaffirming the cultural and artistic spirit of the publishing industry. We aim to do this by presenting bold works of literary merit, each book, individually and collectively, providing a sonic progression that we believe to be too loud to ignore.

TwoDollarRadio.com

Proudly based in
**Columbus
OHIO**

🐦 @TwoDollarRadio

📷 @TwoDollarRadio

f /TwoDollarRadio

SOME RECOMMENDED LOCATIONS FOR READING:
Pretty much anywhere because books are portable and the perfect technology!

COVER PHOTO→   August Friedrich Albrecht Schenck, *Anguish* c. 1878, oil on canvas, 151.0 x 251.2 cm, National Gallery of Victoria, Melbourne, Purchased, 1880 (p.307.6-1).

Page 44: "Zaspeevaymeh Sobee" ("Let's Sing"), http://lemko.org/lih/music/kruzhoks.html; **Page 118:** "Stravinsky – Once At A Border (Full Film) | Tony Palmer Films." YouTube, uploaded by Gonzo Music TV, Jul 6, 2018, https://youtu.be/VK-CUOYw9yuc; **Page 174:** "The Pine is Burning, All Aglow," Steve Repa translation on LyricsTranslate.com; **Page 181:** Walker, Shaun, et al. "Malaysia Airlines Flight MH17 Crashes in East Ukraine." *The Guardian*, Guardian News and Media, 17 July 2014, www.theguardian.com/world/2014/jul/17/malaysia-airlines-plane-crash-east-ukraine; **Page 239:** Carroll, Oliver. "Ukrainian Film Maker Oleg Sentsov Ends 145-Day Hunger Strike in Russian Jail." *The Independent*, Independent Digital News and Media, 5 Oct. 2018, www.independent.co.uk/news/world/europe/oleg-sentsov-hunger-strike-end-russian-jail-ukraine-filmmaker-siberia-a8569901.html; **Page 299:** "Dear Mother Don't Cry," Steve Repa translation on LyricsTranslate.com.

For Bethany

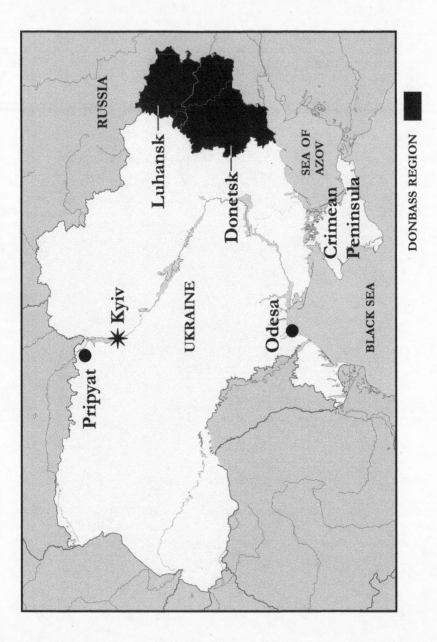

RUSSIA

Luhansk

Donetsk

SEA OF
AZOV

Crimean
Peninsula

Kyiv

UKRAINE

Odesa

BLACK SEA

Pripyat

DONBASS REGION

Timeline of Events at Euromaidan, The Revolution of Dignity, 2013–2014

2013

Nov. 21 — The fourth president of Ukraine, President Viktor Yanukovych, declines to sign an Association Agreement with the European Union, instead chosing to build closer ties with Russia.

Nov. 22 — 2,000 protestors gather in Kyiv's Maidan Nezalezhnosti, Independence Square, to protest, growing to 50,000–200,000 protestors by Nov. 24th.

Nov. 30 — The Ukrainian special police force, the Berkut, attack unarmed protestors and neighboring civilians.

Dec. 1 — As a result of police violence the night before, riots break out and government opposition parties occupy the Trade Unions Building. A tent city goes up at Maidan Nezalezhnosti and a national strike begins.

Dec. 8 — The March of Millions: 500,000 Ukrainians march on Kyiv. A statue of Vladimir Lenin is toppled and destroyed.

Dec. 11 — As 4,000 Berkut attack protestors, the bells at St. Michael's Golden-Domed Monastery ring in alarm for the first time in 800 years.

Dec. 12–28 — Yanukovych and Russian President Vladimir Putin sign the Ukrainian-Russian action plan. Barricades and tents at Maidan Nezalezhnosti reach full capacity with crowds reaching 200,000.

2014

Jan. 10–16 — The Ukrainian Parliament, Verkhovna Rada, passes strict laws against public assembly and protesting, nicknamed "Dictator Laws."

Jan. 19–25 — Riots erupt against the anti-protest laws on Hrushevsky Street, which come into effect on Jan. 21. Water cannons, Molotov cocktails, rubber bullets, and live ammunition are used on protestors, killing 4 people and injuring 1,000.

Feb. 6 — A package delivered to the Trade Unions Building labeled "Medicine," explodes.

Feb. 18–19 — Euromaidan protesters are met with live and rubber ammunition, grenades, and tear gas in an attempt to restrain protesters. Snipers and Berkut with AK-47 assault rifles fire on civilians. Yanukovych refuses to accept a cease-fire. Ukraine goes into a de facto state of emergency. Over 103 civilians and 13 police are killed; 184 citizens sustain gunshot wounds and over 750 citizens are injured.

Feb. 21 — Maidan protestors honor the Heavenly Hundred.

Feb. 22 — Yanukovych flees Ukraine and seeks asylum in Russia. The Verkhovna Rada votes 328–0 to remove Yanukovych from office and sets May 25 as the date for a new presidential election.

Feb. 27–Mar. 18 — Masked pro-Russian troops seize the parliament of Crimea, followed by armed military troops without insignia. By Mar. 18, Crimea has been annexed to the Russian Federation, though it is unrecognized by most international states.

Apr. 7 — Pro-Russian activists storm government buildings in the Donbass region of Ukraine, which includes Donetsk and Luhansk, an action the Ukrainian government denounces as terrorism and a Russian operation to thwart Ukraine independence.

May 11 — Crimean filmmaker Oleg Sentsov is accused of terrorist conspiracy by the Russian government and is arrested.

May 25 — Petro Poroshenko is elected the fifth president of Ukraine.

May 26–27 — First Battle of Donetsk Airport.

July 17 — Malaysian Airlines Flight 17 from Amsterdam to Kuala Lumpur is shot down by pro-Russian separatists while flying over Donetsk Oblast. All 283 passengers and 15 crew members are killed.

August 10 — The last barricades and residential tents are removed by plainclothes Kyivans.

The War in Donbass remains ongoing.

I know that far away
By strangers in a foreign land
I will be laid away;
This little pinch of native soil
Will on my grave be placed —

—Taras Shevchenko

You have navigated with raging soul
Far from the paternal home,
Passing beyond the seas' double rocks.
And now you inhabit a foreign land.

—Medea

I Will Die in a Foreign Land

PROLOGUE
ENTER KOBZARI, SINGING

Where does it begin? Ah, ah. Depends on who you ask—

It could begin with Scythians and Cimmerians, Slavs and the Rus'. Queen Olha. Vladymyr the Great. Yaroslav the Wise.

It could begin with Kyi. Ilya Muromets. The *Kozaks*, the UNR, the UPA. One thing is certain: it doesn't just begin here, my friend. It doesn't begin or end with Stalin. It doesn't begin or end with Yanukovych. Or Poroshenko. Or Zelensky. It doesn't begin or end with Putin.

The war has always been quiet: like a pulse, it can be forgotten. Unnoticed. Like a pulse, we can feel it as long as we're still here.

Lean your ear onto the chest of a corpse and you'll hear it: emptiness like an echo.

Have you ever listened to your wristwatch when it's stopped ticking? The sound of it—that aching hollowness. Like a dry fountain cracking in the sun.

We've known thirst. We've known hunger, here.

Ah, ah. My friend. You ask us where to begin—how can we? How many times have you carried your dead through your streets?

We sing the history of Kyiv: *Come, and you will see.*

THE CAPTAIN

He wakes in his apartment: a bed, a desk, a kitchenette, a radio. The upright piano, a black polished Diederichs Frères elaborately carved in the fashion of the late nineteenth century, stands against an otherwise bare wall. The bearish piano faces him when he emerges from the bedroom, goes to the bath. When he washes his face—dry soap and cold water—he sees the ancient image of his own father, gone so many years ago.

The young people in Kyiv have come to protest abuses of their government—he heard them, saw them gathering in the street. He doesn't remember when exactly the thought came to him, but he remembers putting on his father's Soviet jacket and the balaclava to cover his face, and he quite simply went. The square was filled with people singing, holding hands, holding up the Ukrainian flag: blue bar atop yellow bar. The open sky over the golden grain. The women wore flowers in their hair, the men flowers on their jackets—their hope contagious, he cut through the crowd uplifted and exhilarated with purpose.

This feeling, he recalls, *this feeling—this is how it all began.*

The street piano was where it always had been—there on Khreshchatyk, where he would play day after day. Abandoned by some unknown donor, the light oak top—board bent from weather, the epoxy chipped and worn. He wipes the seat of snow, lifts the cover to expose the white teeth. He warms his hands with his breath, his gloves black with the fingers cut. He twists the ring on his finger, his father's silver ring.

A crowd gathers as he begins to play.

PART I

PART I

МАЙДАН
MAIDAN

UNITY DAY: PROTESTORS KILLED IN KYIV, UKRAINE

JANUARY 22, 2014

Two activists were shot and killed and a third is in critical condition on Wednesday during non-violent demonstrations in the capital city of Ukraine. The protests began on November 21, 2013, after President Viktor Yanukovych declined to sign an association agreement with the European Union and instead considered joining the Eurasian Economic Union, building closer ties to President Vladimir Putin of Russia. Thousands of Ukrainians responded to the move by gathering in the city square, citing governmental corruption and Yanukovych's abuses of power. Protestors also voiced resistance to Russian influence. Ukraine, which has been an independent country since 1991 following the fall of the Soviet Union, has a long, complex history with Russia, resulting in distrust, especially from younger generations of Ukrainians.

The two deaths are the first reported at Maidan Nezalezhnosti, or Independence Square. The Berkut Police Force have been criticized globally for their violent response to the protests, which has included the use of stun grenades, tear gas, batons, and cutting off cell phone communications. Despite these brutal attacks, the number of protestors at Independence Square has only grown in size—many protestors camping in tents and building barricades to protect themselves against the police force.

Journalists covering the unrest in Ukraine have also been targeted. Ukrainian journalist Ihor Lutsenko, 35, was abducted from a hospital along with protestor Yury Verbytsky, 50. Lutsenko was discovered 12 hours later, wandering the crest of a forest on the outskirts of Kyiv near Borispol Airport. Barely able to walk, Lutsenko had been beaten on the soles of his feet, had a black eye, and was missing a tooth. Lutsenko believed the 10 men who abducted him were affiliated with the Berkut Police, stating the men repeatedly asked him who had paid him to participate in the protests—presuming Lutsenko had been provided compensation from Western organizations. He had not.

Not far from where Lutsenko was discovered, so was the body of Verbytsky. He had been bound, ribs broken and internal organs smashed. The autopsy indicated that Verbytsky had died of hypothermia.

The deaths have caused further outrage and protests throughout the country.

ST. MICHAEL'S GOLDEN-DOMED MONASTERY
JANUARY 19, 2014
MORNING

The snow in Boston, Katya thinks, must be thick like cake. She flicks her cigarette. A black cloud of burning tires near the Maidan less than a mile away forces a cough. The air is frigid. The injured have not rested. The light outside is disappearing.

St. Michael's appears to be inside an apocalyptic snow globe: golden spirals, eye-blue walls, ember and ash ethereal. The bell tower stands like a soldier. Indeed, it is.

We're all under water here, Katya thinks. Shaken loose like silt. An undertow. A baptism. A drowning. Last spring, Boston had a bombing. Now, she was in Kyiv.

Kyiv had been burning for months. The tactical police force—the Berkut—had started attacking thousands of peaceful protestors at the Maidan in November. St. Michael's opened its doors, bells ringing and priests singing, and the people came from Maidan to the church. Hundreds had been injured; some were dead. Distrust of the government caused hospitals to turn up in the streets. In shoe stores, in the Hotel Ukraine. In St. Michael's Golden-Domed Monastery.

Here, Katya is far from home.

The holy men of the church—men of all faiths—start to pray, to hold a vigil. They took the bodies to a makeshift morgue in the back of the church and the people prayed. *God is still here,* they said. They said: *Pray.* Vigilance. Vigilance. Stay awake.

Katya's son, Isaac, would have been six years old and still cherub-faced. Ezra had sent her an email that she hadn't yet read. Katya looks at her phone, the message from her husband.

A priest calls out to her—

лікар, будь ласка—

Doctor, please—

Katya kills the cigarette under her boot and goes.

All empires fall. First the Mongols destroyed parts of the church. Then the Soviets. Then it was rebuilt. Gold and blue, the church is grotesquely beautiful. It looks like Byzantium. Byzantium: the word so full of promise. The new Rome. She has seen pictures of the Sistine Chapel and it must be something like this. Here, there are paintings on the walls, the ceiling, the columns. Bright sashes and wings on cherubs, gowns and crowns decorating saints. All looking, seeing. Vigilance. She felt they could see every part of her. All that raw ache.

Inside the church among the injured, an old Soviet man is dying. He wears a military jacket with Soviet insignia sewn upside down. His skull is bleeding underneath the black balaclava he wears, covering his face. Katya takes off her winter coat. A nurse takes it from her and directs her on to the washroom. The medics here all wear white shirts with the Red Cross taped on the chest, on their helmets. Above them hundreds of saints look down, their large heavy eyes watching, their hands lifted to God. Men and women are huddled on the ground under the paintings, under the gold chalices. They are young and old. They pray, crossing themselves. A circle of older women, their heads covered in scarves, pray under a portrait of the Virgin. Katya walks past.

The Soviet man has been moved from the floor to a make-shift operating table. He is stripped of his balaclava, his pants and shoes. His leg is soaked in blood—shrapnel thick inside the thin skin. When she removes the mask she can see he's been blinded by a powder, his eyes closed, tears trailing down his cheeks, rinsing grime from his face. He has a traumatic brain injury and is showing signs for stroke. Katya dresses for surgery, amidst the wailing people, the watchful saints. She covers her mouth, her hands. The nurse crosses herself and says a prayer. They go to work.

The blanket beneath the old man had become wet with blood and there is nothing she can do until he is put to sleep. The wounds isolated. The anesthesia pushed into the skin and he's out. She takes the old man's wrist and feels the faint *beat beat beat.*

She says to him in Russian: "You are a strong man. You can make it through."

Once she's removed the shrapnel, Katya and the nurse muster a tourniquet, ceasing the bleeding. His leg is raised. An IV pinched into the veins of his left arm. Alkaline, lidocaine, corneal gel applied to the eyes. Katya calls for a blanket and she's given one by a nurse. The nurse had taken it from a dead man a few feet away. She had covered the dead man with a sheet. The nurses help her wrap the old man in the blanket and Katya understands he is soon going to die.

She watches the old man's chest. It rises.

Hours later, Katya and a nurse examine the bandages, the blood pressure. The sheets, the walls, the bandages are white.

He says, slurring, trembling from the cold: *Кіса. Kisa.* It means: *Kitten.*

Katya is struck by the strangeness of it: a pet name? A pet?

Isaac would play in the snow until he shook like a bird. He sat on her lap in fleece pajamas after she had him take a warm bath. Katya wrapped the blanket around them both and breathed. They sat by the fire and Katya smelled his hair as she read to him stories.

Today, her son would have been six years old.

Katya pulls back her hair. She washes her hands. Above the sink, Mary holds baby Jesus and watches Katya splash water on her face. Katya looks up.

In the Bible, Simeon says to Mary on the death of Jesus: "And a sword will pierce your own soul too." Mary knew what she was getting into.

What kind of fucking sacrifice is that?

KATYA DREAMS OF HER SON

She sees her boy's prints in the snow—like a rabbit to be tracked. She runs.

The prints go from the sidewalk to the street to the wood. She calls for him and the wood is silent. She hears her own heart in her ear and holds her breath to listen.

She hears him laugh, and she sees the smoke from the hut. She opens the door.

An old woman is at the small stove—long-nosed and crooked. Her legs are chicken legs. She turns the mortar and pestle and she cries out: *Oh, you are too late, my dear. You're too late.* And the old woman points to a door.

Inside is her son, hanging from his feet. Framed paintings of sad byzantine eyes line the wall floor to ceiling. Her son is pale, his arms crossed over his chest.

The old woman comes in with a warm bowl and a spoon and says, *Oh, my dear. Such a ripe little heart.* She hands her the bowl and it begins to beat in her cupped hands.

KATYA'S APARTMENT
JANUARY 20, 2014
DAWN

Katya wakes, gasping for air, as if emerging from the sea. She turns on the bedside lamp and puts on her glasses—the black framed glasses she only wears at home—the glasses only her husband and her son would see her wear. She pulls off the covers and walks barefoot to the window, which she unlatches, and lets in the icy air. She unevenly lights a cigarette, shaking from the wind, from her own unsteady hand, and she blows the smoke into the cold.

At Beth Israel shortly after the bombing, the injured had arrived, shrapnel from the pressure cooker bombs—nails, ball bearings—seared deep in flesh, the limbs, debris blinding the eyes. The emergency room was always an environment of chaos, but at once Katya and every living soul in Boston, a people of formidable hardiness, found themselves off-balance. It was the most terror Katya had ever experienced inside the hospital, besides the death of her son, and her survival of both had instilled such profound intrepidness within her that she was led here to Kyiv: a city on fire. A country verging on war.

The word *Ukraine* means *country*. As if it were the only one. As if there wasn't another place to be from. But what if there isn't? What if it's all one country—this whole world.

I'm a child of the world. Not one country to belong to. Not one mother, or father.

From her apartment window, she can see the barricades burning. She thinks of her mother when she sees the *babusi* handing out handmade scarves and soup. She is her adoptive mother, the mother of her whole-life memory. Her dear mother waits for Katya to return to Boston, to remedy her broken marriage.

Katya has no picture of her birth mother, no name. She has no lead. Like many orphans, she pictures her birth mother as eternally young and beautiful. She pictures her in black-and-white, like the pictures she's seen of her adoptive mother as a girl, except this mother will look like her. Katya emails her mother every day, however brief, to tell her she is safe.

Katya as a child would look at herself in the mirror, long curled brown hair, dark eyes, and speak to the reflection. *She would look just like me,* she'd think. *She'd even talk like me.* And Katya would open her small mouth and say to herself, to the mother's blood inside of her, *My name is Katya. What is your name?* And she'd wait expectantly for the answer, as if her blood-mother somehow possessed her as a spirit.

I miss you, she'd say to her own reflection, eyes round with tears. And as her mother would enter her room to kiss her forehead goodnight, Katya would close her eyes and sometimes pretend—

And feel inside her heart staggering guilt.

Now, in Ukraine, her blood-mother could be anywhere, anyone. She pictures her alive.

"They were troubled," her parents told her, "that they couldn't provide for a child."

"It must have been so difficult," her mother said. "My heart is torn: the poor woman gave her child away, but she gave us you. The night before dawn. The winter before spring."

Ekaterina, her mother and father named her when they took her home from the orphanage. Ekaterina the Great. Looking over Kyiv, Katya feels neither great nor pure. Her son is dead, her marriage is dead, and her birthplace is on fire.

Katya snubs her cigarette on the balcony. A black cat emerges from a bush with a mouse in its jaws. He leaves paw prints in the snow.

Kisa, kisa. Where have you gone?

ST. MICHAEL'S GOLDEN-DOMED MONASTERY
JANUARY 20, 2014
NOON

Amidst the chaos of a new day, the old Soviet man is stable. The nurse sees Katya standing near his bed and joins her, updating her on his progress. The nurse says, "He still exhibits paralysis in his right arm and right leg and non-fluent aphasia."

Katya nods and removes her gloves and coat and looks at the old man, his green eyes light as fog.

"Have we found any identification to call his wife? His family? To tell them where he is?"

"We haven't reached any relatives, yet. There was a phone number in his coat. No answer. There was also a cassette tape."

"Where is it?"

"I put them back in his coat so they aren't lost."

"Okay," she says. "We will keep working on it. He will need some time to recover here—it's too soon for him to leave, but we will need to make room for other patients. Maybe someone will come looking for him, or perhaps he might come around."

She turns back to the old man. He is pale, his hair thinned, his scalp spotted like an egg.

"We are going to move you into the refectory adjacent to this building. It will be quieter there."

He is looking off. Katya tries to see what he does: There are young men around him, covered in blankets with IVs in their wrists and arms. Grimaced faces turned, tucked into their shoulders. The church is the inside of a conch shell: each voice indistinct, the murmur constant.

The old man, though, is looking elsewhere or everywhere at once.

A group of holy men dressed in black gowns begin to sing a hymn. Four of them under the image of Christ. The sound fills the church like a bowl. The voices sound like one voice—low, like an organ, and high. Then, the people in the church start to sing, too. They sing the Ukrainian anthem. The sick sing, the doctors and nurses sing. Prayers and pleas harmonize the same. The music reverberates, between the walls, between the bodies, living and dead.

It feels like a swell, Katya thinks—*like we're drowning. In grief, in ecstasy.*

Where had she heard this before? Why does it keep coming back?

We're all underwater, here, she thinks.

She leaves the old man, who is unable to speak.

Katya asks a volunteer where they have piled his things. Katya can hear the bells, the praying, the crying—a ringing headache, and she pockets a bottle of aspirin from a table. There have been beatings on Hrushevsky Street. The injured are carried in. The volunteer assisting Katya came from Kharkiv. Katya can't remember her name.

"Here," the volunteer says, hands her a plastic bag of the old man's clothes. Katya pulls out the coat. No name, but a Soviet military pin and a piece of paper on the inside pocket near the breast. An American number and address in faded ink on soft yellowed paper. Los Angeles, California. The address seems bizarre, out of place. Foreign in a foreign place. Inconceivable. She gives the volunteer back the coat, where it is lain in a neat pile as it was before.

Katya reaches for her phone but a young woman stops her. The woman is wearing a green coat, hair dyed blond and blue. She grabs Katya's arm.

"Please," she says. "He is hurt—doctor, please—"

Her head splitting, Katya blinks. *Everyone is hurt*, she wants to say. Instead, putting her phone and the paper away in her pocket, she says, "Where is he?" and follows the young woman outside.

It looks as if there has been a war here, a battle. Blood on the cobblestone. Volunteer medics, women carrying gloves and soup—everyone is shouting orders, everyone is running. Only the dead are still.

Outside the monastery, under a tree skeletoned from winter, Katya sees the man—his head and hand bleeding. He's older than she expected—closer to her own age, later thirties, early forties. The young woman goes to him, waves over Katya, who kneels down in the snow.

"*Dobriy dehn*," she says in Ukrainian to the man. "Could you—"

"Go," he says, waving at her. "I'm fine, I'm fine. Please go help the others."

Katya looks at the woman, who tells her, "A Berkut struck him in the head with an iron baton—tell me that isn't serious."

"I had on a helmet," he says, and yes, there it is—the painted helmet cracked in the snow.

"Please," the young woman says to Katya. "He's a fucking idiot."

Katya looks around her, at the people hurting around her, at all the people dying.

"Go," he says in Ukrainian. "Go, please."

She looks him in the eyes. She can recognize a selfless man. A long time ago, she had recognized that quality in Ezra.

"Let me see," she says. He moves his hand from his head. His palms are dirty and calloused. Strong.

"I will ask you some questions, now," Katya says. "What is your name?"

"Misha Tkachenko."

"What year is it?"

"Twenty fourteen."

"Who is president?"

He looks at her—"No one."

"Okay, then. Where did you grow up?"

"Pripyat—No, Dnipropetrovsk. Dnipropetrovsk."

Katya looks at the young woman for approval. She nods. Katya examines his skull. She holds two fingers in front of his eyes.

"Follow my fingers," she says. She watches his eyes as they go side to side.

A volunteer brings her bandages, antiseptic, alcohol, aspirin, a water bottle. She takes the man's pulse. *Tha thump tha thump tha thump*—healthy, steady. Katya dresses the wounds herself— one across his palm, one above the eye. She asks him questions about his vision. She makes him follow her hand with his eyes, cold blue. When he takes the aspirin, Katya takes her own.

"You'll want to watch for signs of a concussion. Vomiting, confusion. We can keep you here until you feel well enough."

"No, no," Misha says to her. "I won't take room away from the others."

The young woman thanks Katya and turns back to Misha. She says, "I'm going back."

He becomes serious and caps the bottle of aspirin. He says nothing to her. Feeling the weight of the silence between them, Katya gets up to leave.

"Doctor," he says to her. "What would you tell your sister who won't go home during a war like this? Even when men start killing one another?"

Katya says nothing. The woman laughs, pulls a strand of blue hair from the corner of her mouth.

"Misha," the woman says. "Stop."

Misha doesn't look away from Katya. Katya shifts. Her feet are numb from the position.

"What would you tell her?" Misha asks her again.

Katya looks at her hands and the aspirin.

"Nothing."

The woman stands. She thanks Katya again. Without saying a word to Misha, the woman leaves. Katya rises, Misha rises. He looks the direction where the young woman walked off—toward Maidan.

"She's off to battle," he says, lighting a cigarette. He laughs. "No one can stop her."

"Thank you, doctor," Misha says. He walks off, not in the same direction as the young woman, his stride as heavy as his hands.

When Katya returns to her phone, she calls the American number from the old man's pocket. It only rings, rings, rings.

BELLS RING AT ST. MICHAEL'S MONASTERY FOR THE FIRST TIME IN NEARLY 800 YEARS
SUNG BY KOBZARI

The guelder-rose, or *kalyna* berry, symbolizes the blood of families, the birth of the Universe. At the center of Maidan in Kyiv is a statue of Berehynia, her arms outstretched. She stands where Lenin once stood. Where Lenin later fell.

She is the Mother, the Slavic protector of the hearth. She holds the *kalyna* wreath at the center of Independence Square.

This is where Dascha and Slava fell in love, where Misha built barricades, where Katya meets an old pianist—

This is where protestors sang, holding hands. This is where the Berkut police force fired shots, where Molotov cocktails kissed the brick and mortar, steel and flesh, and opened holes in the earth. Opening the body, letting blood.

Gazing at Berehynia is Archangel Michael, the city's patron saint, holding a shield and sword. A soldier of God.

At St. Michael's Monastery, in December 2013, the church bells scream—a cacophony summoning the city to prepare for battle. The church has only done this once before: 800 years ago, against the Mongols.

And so, the city comes, the Ukrainian nation comes, the Berkut comes, the military comes! Bells ringing like the sound of the *kalyna* and the creation of the Universe—

Come to war, the bells say.
Come.

AUDIO CASSETTE RECORDING
SIDE ONE

When I was a young man, I went to Prague. It was 1968, and we arrived in the city in the bellies of tanks. It was our international duty. But what they didn't tell us is that we were to be ready for war. We were given real bullets and gas masks. This was not child's play, I knew then.

The Czech people weren't cheering for us, like we had imagined they would be. No, they surprised us, and I was afraid. I was a boy then. I wanted to become a good man. You may not believe it, but I still do.

We were lost, our tank was—the people had taken down the names of the street signs so we wandered in the labyrinth of Prague's city center for days. They set fire to our vehicles and we set fire to theirs. It was hell. We couldn't see where we were going with all the fires, the stones and bricks being thrown at us.

It was August and it was hot. Smoke and dust everywhere, choking us. We were given orders to drive toward the Czech radio station—that we needed to shut it down. We raided the building, sending reporters out, waving our guns, all of us covered in dust.

As we left the building, a woman on the street asked me in Russian, *Brother, why?* and I turned to look at her and she was beautiful. She had a red coat, short hair—she was passing by the barricades when she saw what was happening. Maybe she was going to work. Maybe she worked at the station. Whatever it was—it was fated.

I didn't know what to say to her. No one had told us what to say. My commander noticed and pointed his gun at her and told her to move along, and she did, but her eyes didn't leave mine. They haven't, still.

One hundred people died in Prague in 1968. A Czech student lit himself on fire. There were others who followed.

The Czech people—your people, your mother's people—did not see us as liberators. I feared I made a mistake by coming. I dared not write home about it. I dared not speak about it. I held my gun, but I doubted. God, I doubted. It was the first time in my life. It wasn't the last.

I was at the top of my class—strong, tall, like my father. My father was an officer in the army, and I was recruited as an officer in the KGB.

My father. How dearly I wanted to be like him. I wanted to be a good man. I wanted to be a good soldier. I wanted to be a good father.

[Incoherent. A pause.]

I remember what it was I said to her—your mother—the last time I saw her. She was leaving. I said not *stop* but *wait*. I think about this every day.

Wait implies, *stay a while*. A stasis. Limbo.

But *stop*—it means *freeze, don't move*. It means, *don't go*.

Dear child, my daughter, my Anna—I pray you hear me. Don't go. Please.

Until the end, my dear. Please hear me until the end.

MAIDAN NEZALEZHNOSTI
JANUARY 18, 2014

It's never so simple. Ukraine is the Jerusalem of the Slavs: every-one wants a piece, Misha Tkachenko thinks as he crosses himself while walking through the camp at Maidan.

The smoke from burning tires suffocates the square. Just outside Maidan, the city center, the sky is clear. Women and men go to work, to the markets. They go to restaurants and clubs, laugh and make love, but here, the smoke hovers like a fog. Ash has dirtied Misha's forehead. He wears a heavy coat, heavy boots, and wool pants, a balaclava in his pocket.

It's January in Kyiv, and it's fucking cold.

There are supporters outside in the streets, clean-faced people who made simple meals for the protestors at Maidan. Misha has been at Maidan since November, when the college students were beaten in the street. He's set up camp with others. As an engineer, he's helped build barricades, structures made from shoveled snow, fence railings, staircases—whatever steel and wood they can get their hands on. He's carried the injured and he's protected the children who have joined their families.

Misha once saw a father beaten right before his child's eyes. Misha fucking hated that Berkut, the one who took down the man—not just because of the pain inflicted on the father, but because of the memory inflicted on the son. Misha saw to it that the Berkut stopped inflicting pain. He helped the father up and took the boy's hand. The Berkut lay on the pavement, and Misha called for help.

The man's family still comes to Maidan. He goes to see the mother, Galyna, who has brought homemade bread and *kalyna* berry tea. Galyna smiles at him weakly—squeezes his hand every time she sees him. *Everyone here is so goddamn tired. Everyone here knows we have to finish what we started.* Even Galyna. Even Misha.

The *kalyna* tea is a little bitter but the warmth feels nice. The tea makes him think of the berry crowns Slava used to wear at FEMEN protests before the organization moved to France. And the first time he met her, at a play, she was wearing a crown of *kalyna* berries, a crown so large she looked like an Orthodox Saint. Bright hair, large eyes, thin mouth.

A martyr. *Drama queen.*

Still, he admired her. She would go bare-breasted into the street, ribbons in her hair, locking arms with other women, chest painted the colors of the flag. The women of FEMEN were fearless, sharp, volatile. They screamed for women's rights, painted UKRAINE IS NOT A BROTHEL on their bellies. She was often arrested. Coming home, mascara-stained and furious as the sun. He didn't love her foolishness, but the spirit. She was idealistic and fire-eyed.

Slava doesn't talk about FEMEN anymore. There was significant fallout after it was discovered a man pulled the strings of the organization, but Slava did not stay disillusioned. "It wasn't working," she would say. "It was too vain—but the shock of it was exhilarating."

Now, reignited, Slava refuses to leave the streets of Maidan. *It's a bad game,* he thinks. He thinks it because he knows what it's like and he's tried to tell her so many fucking times.

You know life is too short, Misha. You know that. To be angry. That's what Vera would say. What his father might say. *How much energy do we waste being angry at the ones we love?*

Misha finishes his bread and takes his phone out of his pocket. He goes to one of the electronics charging tents. A few other men are there, two on their phones, one on a laptop, and Misha nods to them. They look like soldiers and no one has anything to say today after the shooting. No one wants to speak about the dead.

Misha plugs in his phone, cups the tea, closes his eyes, and waits. He tries to remember the woman on the train when he came to Kyiv. She looked like a vintage Cleopatra—short bangs, severely cut. Serious and dour. Maybe it was Dominika. Viktoria.

Misha had been returning on the train from Donetsk for Vera's funeral. He shared a cabin with the woman. She looked up at him from her magazine, stretched out her leg to touch his. Their eyes locked. She slid her foot up his ankle, his calf, his thigh. Then she knelt, unhooked his belt. Misha said, *Please, I don't have any money.* And she said, *I'm not doing this for you. I'm doing this for my husband, who I left by getting on this train. I want this for me.*

So, she did. And when they were finished, she asked Misha if he wanted to go to a play in Kyiv. Misha, with only a duffel bag and a backpack, uneager to return to his vacant apartment, said, *Okay.*

The play was at an apartment, in a bedroom. It was raining outside and all the windows were open. The balcony was kind of a stage—there were two bedrooms joined to it. The actors changed in the adjacent room and the audience watched them perform in the other.

People were sitting in the room on the floor, on the bed, standing in the hallway. Most of the furniture was missing to make room.

Dominika—*that had to be her name*—she was nice. Dominika brought them both drinks. Wine in a plastic cup. Misha sat down on top of his duffel bag. String lights illuminated and shadowed the ceiling. The play was just in front of the balcony. It was sticky-hot, wet. The place was packed.

Misha found himself claustrophobic, trapped. Knees up to his chest. He was near the door and someone's legs were next to his face. A woman's—she hadn't shaved.

He remembers that was the first time she smiled, *when she sat next to me. She had a pretty smile*, Misha thinks, now, that maybe he should have treated her better. Maybe he should have said *Thank you*, or *Goodbye*.

The lights had gone off, then. Women appeared on the balcony—helpers in the audience used flashlights as stage lights. Bra-less women painted white, all wearing wreaths of flowers. Their chests were painted and they had torn *vyshyvankas* on, exposing bellies, exposing breasts.

Misha hadn't seen a torn *vyshyvanka* before. They're always so clean, pressed. He felt the woman with the legs shift her weight. Dominika didn't drink her wine. Everyone had been still.

A few men came in, then, dressed in Soviet uniforms. They had rifles—some of them were old, some were modern. Misha remembers thinking that they were all going to be shot in the apartment, some kind of massacre. The soldiers pointed their guns at the audience, and people in the room started to shout and a few women even screamed, and then they turned their guns on the women in the *vyshyvankas* and crowns.

The music started, or it was more of a sound than music. Like a pulse, or a deep bass sound. Everything started to shake—the whole place. All the flashlights went everywhere, just strobes of people's faces in the dark, of the soldiers' guns, bodies.

Then the music stopped and all the lights fell on one woman wearing the *kalyna* berry crown, dress torn, small breasts. She had blond hair and black eye makeup streaming down her face. Slava.

She said:
Їсти власних дітей - це варварський вчинок!
Eating your own children is a barbarian act!

All the other actresses lit up before the light fell into a strobe. They started crying, bodies contorted, their arms and legs in angles, jerking. All of them, sucking in their bellies and cheeks, using their fingers to pull on their bellies like they were trying to rip themselves open.

Slava stood still, lifted her arms slow. The soldiers stood beside her while all the other women fell onto the ground, crying, twisting. Then the soldiers lowered their guns, and there was an electric crack. The whole place went black. Everything gone quiet, except for a woman in the audience, crying.

Misha felt like he couldn't breathe. It reminded him of being in the mines. Everything was dark, everything black. He could feel the woman's legs next to him, his back against the wall. It felt like the apartment had collapsed, everyone falling into one another, *everyone falling—*

Misha opens his eyes and gasps for air. It's hot in the tent, and he needs to go outside. He needs to breathe. He's shaking, his head spinning, pulse heavy in his throat. He takes from his pocket two pills and swallows without water.

"You okay?" a man with a laptop asks.

"Yeah," Misha says, looking at his phone, charged just enough. He feels the pills begin to work, untangling him from a braid. He takes his phone, goes back into the cold.

It comes on like that, sometimes. The mines.

Being at Maidan, it gets worse when the military police back them in, when the fires start. Some men lit a Berkut bus on fire, and the smoke choked him, reminded Misha of the sulfur, the soot underground. At Maidan, Misha stays outdoors whenever he can.

He'd only been inside the Trade Unions Building once, when it was first sacked by the protestors, with Slava. A man in a balaclava and a Soviet jacket played the piano on a burned Berkut bus outside the building, and many stopped to sing. It was a strange thing, all those protestors huddled together, their government gone to shit, and they're singing. Slava stopped to sing, too. An old woman next to him said, *His music lifts me*, with her hand on her heart. A group of men in painted helmets, repairing a barricade, stopped to listen.

It had a magic to it—the Maidan. As much as it possessed a terror.

Misha had hoped she'd stay away from Maidan when it became violent, though seeing her believe again in something beautiful, something possible, lifted his spirit. The young people holding hands with painted faces—Slava had been there from the beginning. She looked like she did when she had been with FEMEN—bright eyes, wild smile. She would return to Maidan, and days would pass. Then the Berkut came, and Misha, unable to stay inside his apartment while the rest of the country went to war, while Slava went to war, went out to Maidan.

He knew she didn't love him—they had never been in love with one another—but he hoped he'd be able to bully her, guilt her, like a brother, to stay home. Like a sister, she didn't listen. Hasn't still. And women like Slava, like his mother, and like Vera: he admires them.

When Misha leaves the tent, he inhales the choke of the tires burning. The city center has turned to a refugee camp and he wants to feel something for it, wants to honor what it once was, but he feels nothing at all. His heartbeat, still fearful and airy, quickens.

After two tries, Slava doesn't answer. Misha considers a voice message, but not knowing what to say, never knowing what to say, says nothing. All these fearless women want to kill him, he thinks. He cares for them and he loves them and then they kill him with worry. He tosses his phone on the pavement and crushes it beneath his boot.

SLAVA'S APARTMENT
SHOVKOVYCHNA STREET
JANUARY 18, 2014

Yaroslava Orlyk wakes up to two missed calls from Misha. She tries to call him back twice but there is no answer. She lies in bed, looking at her phone. She has messages from an American journalist with a Biblical name. She met Adam at a club in October, shortly before the protests began.

"Do you dance?" he had asked her in Russian, yelling over the music.

It was his last night in Kyiv—he was an essayist for an important American magazine.

She took him by the arm.

And later, by the collar. By the waist. By the lip.

"Will I end up in your story?" she asked him before he left. He reddened, he laughed.

Now, Slava looks at her phone and the text message reads: *I'll be returning to Ukraine for the protests. I want to see you again.*

Slava, who has seen and felt much hardness in her short life, loved his admiring, eager glances. *This American has sweetness in him,* she thought. She doesn't respond to him, not yet. Instead, she tries to call Misha again, a third time. Still there is no answer.

When she first saw Misha Tkachenko years ago, blue eyes sullen, she wanted to love the sadness out of him.

He didn't tell Slava about his Vera—not right away. She knew he had been married, the ring still on his finger his first night in

Kyiv. It was weeks before Misha told him about Vera and her sickness. This same night he told Slava about his father, and his sickness. His mother. And Slava was struck by how much he loved his family. It was the only time that she had been jealous of Misha. She wished her father had been a good man. She wished her mother had been a good woman. As Misha told her about his family, Slava's fingers traced his belly, the slope of his hip. When he finished, Slava sought his sex, his open mouth.

Slava, little painkiller. Her love like benzodiazepine.

The mind in agony, until Slava helps it relax, relax.

When the sex between them had ended, she called Misha her *velyky brat*—Big Brother. He calls her Little Sister. She wasn't his, he wasn't hers, but they were together. For years now, a cobbled family.

Slava looks at her phone again, wondering if she should call a fourth time. There had been threats of violence at Maidan, and she worries Misha had been hurt—why else would he call?

She gets out of bed, her hair tangled, her bed-dress wrinkled. She showers, brushes her teeth, dresses, and ties her hair on top of her head. She ties her boots and a rancorous banging shakes her front door, causing her heart to rise to her throat. She waits, waits, and she hears her name, Slava, and with only one boot on she opens the door to a bull of a man—Misha Tkachenko, hot with rage and panic.

"I called you," he says, "twice, and you didn't answer."

"I called you back," Slava yells, "and you didn't answer."

"I killed my phone," he yells. "What's the point if no one I call answers it."

"And instead you come here and yell at me? What the hell is wrong with you, Misha?"

Misha paces in the hallway of Slava's apartment, breathing through his nose like a steer, and she can see he's panicked.

"Misha," she says, softly. "Misha, take off your boots and come inside. I can make breakfast."

She goes to him and helps him take off his coat. She hugs him by the waist and they go into the kitchen, where Slava makes eggs. Misha goes to the balcony and smokes. It's quiet. It's still early. Sirens, though—still sirens screaming.

"Was it the smoke?" Slava asks, bringing two plates. Her phone on the table lights with a message.

"I think so," Misha says. "It chokes, you know, like the sulfur in the mines. I panic."

Slava nods. "Stay here, Misha," she says. He shakes his head, gesturing at the phone.

"I don't want you to meet him."

"Who?"

"The American."

Slava watches him. Neither plate has been touched.

"It's a business exchange. I am an interesting person, a Ukrainian woman, and he is a writer. I live the story, he writes it."

"You know this is stupid, Slava. He doesn't see it that way."

"How does he see it?"

"You will owe him."

"Eventually, he will send me gifts and money because he thinks he's in love with me, and I will give him sex and attention and pretend to be in love with him. It's even."

Misha leans back in his chair, a pack of cigarettes in his hand. He puts one behind his ear. "It's fucking foolish," he says. But he knows he's lost.

Slava remembers a time when she could almost love him as a wife, make a home for him, but that's not the type of woman she is. Mama would have liked that, she thinks. She looks at Misha and thinks even now he is handsome, unshaven, unshowered. He puts the cigarette in his mouth. He stands up, goes to the balcony, lights the cigarette.

"Slava," Misha says. "I'm sorry. I'm overtired." He meets her eye. "And maybe I should keep my mouth shut."

Slava thinks, if she had been a different woman, she would have married this man. In a different life.

SLAVA'S APARTMENT
SHOVKOVYCHNA STREET
JANUARY 18, 2014

Misha lies next to Slava in her bed. It's been more than a year since they've been together like this, since they've made love, since they've kissed. It feels easy, natural, the way of things. Slava's legs reach open toward his, her toes stretching. The sun has gone, and they've made love twice, slept, and showered together. She lies next to him now, turning, looking at him, propped on her elbows.

The Holodomor—he remembers. *That was the name of the play.*

His babusya had written about that time, after she survived it. Their farm was outside Chernobyl, well before Chernobyl existed. Everything was taken by the Soviets. She had eaten rotten potatoes, skinny birds, skinny dogs, skinny cats. They ate grass, drank water until their bellies swelled up.

Years later, as a little girl, Misha's mother found the diary. She read in it about the neighboring farm where they suspected the father ate his child. Misha's mother would avoid the old man after that, when he would wave to her across the garden. Even more, she began to fear her own father. That maybe one day he'd eat her if he got hungry enough.

How much energy does the body use to survive?
How much energy does the body use to kill?

Misha takes a lock of Slava's blue-tipped hair, spooling down a freckled shoulder.

"Do you remember when we first met?" he asks. "That play?"

Slava laughs, "Misha, no. This sentimentality. Have you breathed too much smoke?"

"I was thinking of it at Maidan. I don't know why. Humor me."

"You had just come in from Donetsk. It was your first night in Kyiv. The next day you buried Vera."

"Yes."

He can feel himself getting caught—some kind of sadness overtakes him. Slava sees it, attempts to meet his eye. He puts his hand on her shoulder, tracing a bone with his thumb.

"Kyiv has been home because you have been in it," he says.

Slava attempts a smile. Tears choke her. She puts her hand on his.

"Why all of this, Misha? What's wrong?"

He looks at her hand, takes it.

He says nothing, but the feeling overtakes him. A realization of the end, rising like a wave, a swell, a feeling of drowning. A feeling of letting go. It feels like grief, it feels like mourning.

When he thinks of Vera, she's untouchable. She's untouchable like a dream, like a saint. She still visits him, sometimes. It's not a vision. It's not a memory. It's a feeling, maybe. A feeling of being close, feeling someone love him.

"Misha," Slava says, putting her chin on his shoulder. "Misha, this will be the last time. This will be the last time for us. Okay?"

"I know," he says. Slava kisses his forehead. "Stay tonight," she says, though they both know he will not.

A LEMKO FOLK SONG
SUNG BY KOBZARI

Let's sing together
in two voices.
One will go higher,
the other will go lower.

When two voices
are joined by another,
that will be beautiful
with three voices.

People should not think
that an organ is playing.
In our village,
that is the people singing.

AUDIO CASSETTE RECORDING
SIDE ONE CONTINUED

When I joined the Red Army, every good Soviet boy's hero was Lenin. I was born during Stalin's time, just after the Second World War. My father had been a soldier, then. A decorated officer. I loved my father. To me, he was larger than Lenin, stronger than Stalin. I would play toy soldiers with the other boys at school, and in my private heart I pretended always to be my father.

My father was a handsome, quiet, fearsome man. My mother, young as she was, understood my father. I knew this even as a child. The two of them could be in the same room for hours never saying a word—my mother sewing, my father reading the paper.

The house was peaceful. My mother and father never fought, which meant to me as a child that they loved one another. I never considered that perhaps they were afraid of one another, that maybe they didn't want to know one another, that they had a full life, with a marriage and children raised in the Soviet way, and what else, could there be. The only noise that filled the house was the piano when I played, and the pounding of Anna's feet as she danced. The screams and laughter that she and I made, that filled our bellies and throats, the tears in our happy eyes—it was lovely being a child in my parents' house.

My mother was the one with the gift. She had a soft voice that warbled like a bird, but it was my father who wanted us to learn music. We learned the arts, my father said, to be civilized people because the world was at times a most uncivilized place. I often forgot he survived the war.

I resisted my lessons, postponed them by asking our instructor questions like, *How does the key make a sound?* and *What is a key?* and once my instructor became so flustered and angry that she raised her voice at me and smacked my hands with a ruler and told me to play my scales. My father came to collect me and noticed my reddened fingers.

What is this? my father asked, kneeling down to me, holding my hands. *Have you not been performing well?* he asked me. I shook my head.

He performs very well, the instructor said. *When he chooses to play.* Then she told my father I had asked too many questions.

My father stood, meeting her eye, and asked her, *What type of questions?* and when the piano instructor told him, my father nodded, and without saying a word, touched my back and led me out the door.

My father called the instructor's father, who owned a piano shop. *My son has an interest in learning how music is made. The mechanics interest him as much as the artistic practice.*

A week later the old piano man came to our home. My mother led him to our piano, where I was sitting, waiting. She brought tea and the old man nodded at me. My mother left us.

So, the old man whispered. *Are you ready to learn a bit of magic?*

I nodded and the old man sat beside me on the bench and began to play the keys, testing the pedals. He made some notes in a little book he had brought. When he was finished, he asked me to help him remove the photos and knickknacks off the piano.

I carried my parents' wedding picture, a civil union—a picture of them at the court; the picture of Anna and I as babies, Anna leaning into me and I sitting cross-legged, propping her up. I held them dearly, tenderly placing them on a bare table, removing the doilies my great grandmother had made and folding them with the solemnity of a flag-bearer. The old man smiled at the great care I took and sent me for a chair so I could stand higher—I needed to see inside, he told me. I needed to touch the piano myself in order to learn.

He opened the top of the black upright and I saw the belly of the piano for the first time. He showed me where we needed to unlatch and unscrew the casing of the piano to remove the front, exposing the bottom near the pedals.

It looks like a harp, I told the old man.

Do you know the bandura, Aleksandr? he asked me.

It's like a guitar, I said, *or a harp*.

Yes, good. The bandura was used by Kobzari *to sing* dumy—*epic tales in verse. Do you know the* Kobzari*?* I shook my head. The old man turned to his satchel and took out the tools, one by one.

The Kobzari *were storytellers*, he said. *Musicians, singers. These men were oftentimes blind—they would sing in their native language, Ukrainian, and it angered the tsar. They were killed, they were banned.*

Why were they killed? I asked.

Because the Kobzari *performed for the common people. The rulers called them useless, brushed them off, ignored them—but they also called them dangerous because they challenged the ideas of the tsar.* The old man watched me and selected one of his tools.

Music, Aleksandr. It is a powerful, dangerous thing. He smiled, holding a strange tool that looked like an inverted screwdriver. *We must do all we can to protect it.*

The old teacher taught me how to fix the piano, week after week. Anna came home from her dancing lessons to find me under the piano with the old man, testing the pedals, replacing the strings. Slippered and pink in her leotard from the heat of the studio, she knelt beside me and watched us work, and then she'd leave us alone.

My father paid for the materials but the old man waived the labor and the lessons. The old man never spoke about the *Kobzari* when others were around.

With me, he spoke of the mechanics, the way the hammer would strike the string, creating a sound. He told me about the sound of the universe, how the Buddhists, Vedics, Jains believed the mantra *Om* was the first vibrational sound within a being when the universe was created. The sound is made of the three deities: Brahma, Vishnu, and Shiva.

Nada Brahma means, *God is sound. Nada*, for vibration, and *Brahma*, for God.

The old teacher taught me these things and I understood that what he was teaching me while tuning the piano was sacred, was secret, was more important than anything I had ever learned before.

Until I learned again to trust. Until I met Jarmila. Jara.

Love, Aleksandr, the old man said to me on our first day, *is holy in all languages, in all religions. 'God is Love.'*

God isn't real, I said.

The old man smiled at me. He said, *That is what you believe, then?*

I nodded.

The old teacher went back to the piano, and as he played, he taught me that the Hebrews believed in the harmony of the spheres—the planets analogous to musical pitches, spaced in just the same way as ratios to musical intervals in tone. Seven planets, seven tones.

The Pythagoreans, by way of Aristotle, by way of my piano teacher, said: *The whole heaven is a musical scale and number.*

This old teacher taught me music. He taught me about God. He warned me about the power of love.

In Soviet times, it was dangerous to believe in God, and it was dangerous to love. Some love is okay—the love of Lenin, of Stalin—but there's a certain type of love that can kill you. A deeper kind. A kind that possesses, disorients. The love of family is dangerous enough. But then there's a kind of love that when discovered, wants to survive like a disease, and it will ruin you as you try to protect it.

The damn torture of it all, my sweet, my darling—I can't remember the dear old man's name.

ST. MICHAEL'S GOLDEN-DOMED MONASTERY
JANUARY 24, 2014

Misha Tkachenko has been at the monastery helping the wounded. When Katya arrives in the morning he is there and when she goes home, he's still there. Maybe he disappears for a meal somewhere, but he's been there, in gentle spirits. She likes having him. He can speak to people unlike a doctor, unlike a medic. He has been at Maidan the whole time so he knows what to say. He is easy, friendly, making the injured laugh.

He is also, though, incredibly serious and tender. Gripping the shoulder of a man, giving him courage. Holding the hands of an old woman praying over a young dead man. Katya finds herself looking for him because to see him brings her comfort. He brings everyone comfort.

Misha has been spending time with the old man. He calls him the Captain. The old man has had many visitors who bring him small gifts and pray over him. For many, this is the first time they are seeing his face.

"You haven't heard of this man?" Misha had asked Katya, days ago, seeing the Captain's visitors crowd around him.

"This is who I now call the Captain, but he is known as the Pianist of Maidan."

"Pianist of Maidan?"

"Every day he came to Independence Square to play. He wears this old coat, a balaclava. He is something of a hero."

"I did not realize—does anyone know his name? He wears a wedding band. Has anyone ever seen him, or heard him, speak about his wife?"

"Not a soul. Those who could get close to him said he had brown eyes, but I see now they have flecks of green. He keeps his distance."

"Then it is your task to find out his name," she had said, and went on her way.

She hasn't tried the number again. The Captain doesn't know she has it, that she keeps it in her pocket with the cassette. She had told Misha about the tape, who offered to bring an old player he had. But the Hrushevsky Street riots have pulled their attention away—protestors had been trapped by military barricades while the police force fired upon them. The president gave the police medals for their valor. Still, protestors show up in the street, and because the hospitals are not safe, they arrive wounded at the church. There are not enough nurses, so Katya has taught Misha how to wrap a bandage, how to properly clean a cut, how to stop the bleeding on an open palm. The two of them drift apart, like two boats caught in a tide, helping as many people as they can manage.

Now, in the constant flood of her duties, Katya realizes she has forgotten to check in on the Captain and has lost sight of Misha. She rushes to the refectory and is relieved to find them both. Misha is speaking Russian to the old man. The Captain appears calm, comfortable, but still unable to talk. She smiles as the Captain laughs with Misha by his side, and Katya thinks maybe the old man will live.

She imagines the Captain dressed in a nice brown suit, a cap. Maybe a limp from the injury he's sustained. A cane. Shiny leather shoes, cleanly shaven. She imagines him going for coffee at a café, and a younger person is there—a son or daughter. She imagines them seeing one another for the first time after some time apart. She can't imagine anything beyond the initial reunion. It gets foggy. But there's a feeling—this kind of warmth that takes over, and she feels hopeful.

She feels hopeful that the next time she calls the number, someone will pick up. She thinks about that echo, the waiting on the other side of the line. She had waited, and waited, then the line dropped. Silence. Like space between breath.

She thinks of Isaac, for an instant. The letter from Ezra she's read thirty times:

Come home, Ezra wrote. *Please, come home.*

The thought of her home in Boston, the heavy lock turning, the springed screen door against her back, freeing herself from muddy boots on the entry. A scarf tangled in her hair and purse, she'd hang her coat between Ezra's thick black wool pea coat and Isaac's blue puffed jacket. The house would smell like cinnamon in the winter, and salt in the summer. She'd hang the keys on the hook and Isaac would run to her, another fourteen-hour day, another surgery, another recovery—*Mama, Mama*—feet thumping like a crooked heartbeat.

Tha thump, thump thump, tha thump.

But in Ukraine the sun is fading and Katya is faint with hunger. She had been working on a man who'd been shot in the back, near the shoulder. He had been looking better, healthier. So close to the heart, she thinks, examining his wound. Some of us are fortunate. As she goes to wash her hands, Misha approaches her.

"How are you, doctor?" he says.

She smiles weakly at him. "So-so. I needed to rest. Just a little time."

Misha nods, understanding. He says with a faint smile, "So, you're not superhuman?"

Katya dries her hands and looks at him, smiling back. "You seem to be here every day. Laughing. Helping."

Misha shrugs. "It's not much."

"It is," she says. "I'm an American doctor. I'm not trusted the same way you are. It brings people comfort. It's a gift."

He shrugs again. Then, "I thought your Ukrainian sounded a little funny."

"Yes," she says. "I was born in Kopachi village but grew up in the United States."

"*Kopachi?*"

"Yes."

"Huh," he says, crossing his arms, looking at her. Examining.

"My grandmother's farm is in Opachychi. Not far," he says. "We were neighbors, in a way. Our families. I grew up in Pripyat—so, not far. Well. For a time."

Katya says nothing.

He senses her insecurity. He goes on to ease her. "I'd been meaning to ask you—the Captain?"

Katya looks at her hands. "He is very hurt."

Misha leans into her, nearly touching. "Doctor, will he live through this?"

Katya smooths her jacket, sighs. She looks over at the old man, who has dozed off. She doesn't know what she feels for him. Some kind of tenderness.

"It isn't up to us," she says.

"What about the tape? Should we listen to it?"

"It's not for us," Katya says. Misha nods, looks over to the sleeping Captain. Katya realizes she's not the only one with that feeling of tenderness.

"Will you be here long, doctor?" he asks her.

"Katya," she says, smiles politely. "My name. I'll be here as long as I'm needed. Until the protests end."

"Katya. What about tonight? Will you be here long?"

She realizes she doesn't know the time.

"Have you eaten?" he asks her, and Katya laughs.

"No," she says. "Maybe I should."

"Please," Misha says, "let me find you something."

Katya puts her hands up in protest, but Misha waves her away and disappears beyond the monastery door.

MAIDAN NEZALEZHNOSTI
JANUARY 24, 2014

There had always been music in the streets surrounding Maidan during the protests. When everything was peaceful, Misha would join with them, bringing his guitar. The people made a circle.

A circle makes a harmony.

A circle spins and spins, like a cog.

The wheels on a minecart.

Go, sing. Go—

In the beginning he only came out in the evenings, after work. He started to teach a young college student how to play the guitar, meeting every night near the fountain and showing him the shapes of the chords. When things became violent, Misha lost track of the boy—named Oler. He had nothing else—not a family name, or an address. They just disappeared from one another as naturally as they came.

How much energy does it take to look for something you'll never find?

As he looks for a meal for Katya, he sees the piano, painted blue and gold, on top of a burned Berkut bus. A new pianist plays, his face painted blue, his hands exposed to the cold. He plays because the Captain cannot. He wears a bulletproof vest and fatigues. The Captain would always play from memory, but this pianist has sheets of music. As the pianist plays, a few people hover over his shoulder, singing.

Misha lights a cigarette. When the pianist finishes the song, he yells to the crowd: *Long Live the Captain, Glory to the Heroes!*

It has been nearly three months that the Ukrainian people have been protesting in Kyiv. Too many have died. Too many have been injured. Misha nods at the homage to the Captain. Misha will tell him his presence is missed.

When Misha went back to work in the mines in Donetsk and left Vera in Kyiv, she started taking piano lessons. It had been so long since she played, she said, and she could use the company. Once she found a teacher, she would record the lessons on a tape recorder and save them. She grew attached to the recorder, and because their phone calls were never able to last long, between the lessons she would record her own voice, telling Misha about her day, her thoughts, her wishes. She talked about the news, the friends she saw—recording their mutual friends' voices as they all sat together at dinner, at a café. She would send these recordings to him through the mail while he was away working in Donetsk. Misha would listen to them over and over, warm and drunk, until he fell asleep.

Now it is fifteen below. The crowd has dispersed. The pianist stands with his friends, smoking. Without the piano, the silence is crisp and loud and bright in the cold.

He begins to wonder what Katya would like to eat, what would be best for her, what might give her strength. He likes the idea of helping Katya—her serious brow and careful hands. He's been paying attention to her, how she's been working with her patients. She's measured. Even. He enjoys her steady grace, her natural ease.

Unlike Vera—who was sensitive, ethereal, birdlike—there is no frailty in Katya. Katya is a small woman, but there was a hardiness to her—a wise, sensual, soulful awareness, both corporeal and otherworldly. And yes, a sweetness.

She's from Chernobyl, he thinks, and as he considers a meal for her, he's struck by the desire to please her. He finds a cup of soup—a perfect meal—and a hot cup of tea.

For so long, Misha has felt useless, maimed. *It feels good*, he thinks. He means, *Helping*. He does not like to think of Vera but he does. Especially now. Especially when he helps Katya. He remembers Vera close to the end. How light she was when he lifted her. Her delicate bones like lace. Her skin gossamer. So airy that if he breathed, she might float away.

Misha heads back to the church, the golden-domed monastery. St. Michael watches him cross the square. The pianist has returned on the Berkut bus and begun playing the national anthem. The crowd is singing. Misha moves past them, the sound of the voices encouraging, propelling him. He sees Katya walking out of the church into the snow to meet him. He gives her the soup, the heat from it brightening her cheeks, watering her eyes. Behind her the thin sound of the voices rises from the church, singing a hymn.

Katya smiles. Misha, too.

"Glory to Ukraine," she says, raising her soup.

"Glory to Ukraine," he says, then, "Long Live our Captain."

Months later, in the ruins of an airport, Misha Tkachenko will remember this moment with Katya. It will be warm and the sun will be hot, but somewhere inside him, before he finishes his cigarette, Misha will still feel the cold in Kyiv.

Katya will remember while sitting at a café with her husband in Boston. She will be looking at her husband's hands, tearing a sugar packet into pieces. The sun will reflect off a passing car, blinding her for an instant. Neither she nor Ezra will speak. Katya will look away, remembering a dream.

Ah, ah—
But, for now:
Misha burns his tongue on the tea. Katya burns her tongue on the soup.
Katya smiles at Misha, unsure why. Misha smiles back, unsure how.

The hearts of the holy men burst, beaming up to Christ.
The crowds outside and inside the church raise their voices to Ukraine.
Berehynia raises the guelder-rose and St. Michael raises his sword.

All the while, the Captain hums out of tune, not knowing the words.

My old piano teacher said to me, *If you want to make God laugh, tell him your plans. Good thing I don't believe in God*, I said. He laughed.

If there is a God, I don't think he laughs. We like to think he does—that he has a sense of humor, that he is like us, *made us in his image*—but I think he is God because he's nothing like us. He is Alpha and Omega.

God is who He is because He is Reason—the Judge.
A Great Scale, measuring us. He is The Maker.
In the beginning was the Word
and the Word was with God
and the Word was God.

Logos—the Word. Logic, Reason.

The Latin Bible bends to *Logos*. The Orthodox, *Hagia Sophia*. Wisdom. The two are not the same and yet we treat them the same.

The Bible says, *A person may think their own ways are right, but the Lord weighs the heart.* The heart—is it true the heart is the same size as a fist? I've known men who would tear out my heart to see just how much it weighed, the size of it, whether it bled Red.

The Bible also says *God is Love. God is Light.* Love and Light. The love that has no bounds. God the Father.

God, how I couldn't wait to become a father. My own father, how his children betrayed him. They buried him and my mother after they came for Anna.

Your aunt Anna, your namesake: the Chosen One.

Do you know *The Rite of Spring? Le sacre du printemps?* I will tell you the story, but no, not yet. In my mind you are still a little child, a little kitten.

But dream on this: we are lions in a den.

ARTISTS AROUND THE WORLD DEMAND THE IMMEDIATE RELEASE OF OLEG SENTSOV

The Ukrainian-Crimean filmmaker was arrested at his home of Simferopol, Crimea, on May 11, 2014. Sentsov, 39, has been accused of plotting terrorist attacks in the region. The *Gamer* filmmaker and father of two was an activist during the Euromaidan protests in Kyiv against President Viktor Yanukovych early this year and has been a vocal opponent in recognizing the annexation of Crimea by the Russian Federation. Sentsov has denied all crimes against him and was last seen in custody in Moscow.

The arrest has fueled outrage around the globe. PEN International, Amnesty International, the European Film Academy, and a number of writers, filmmakers, actors, and artists are taking a public stand with the Ukrainian activist by initiating petitions and using the hashtag #FreeSentsov on social media.

Sentsov faces up to 20 years in prison.

BORYSPIL AIRPORT
OUTSIDE KYIV
JANUARY 22, 2014

The American arrives and Slava is there to greet him at the airport. She stands outside, smoking, listening to the cabbies attempting to swindle rides. One man approaches her, his teeth yellowed and his clothes wrinkled, offering her a fare.

"Too low," she says, and his eyebrows raise. "I am meeting an American. Charge more."

The man laughs and winks at her. He goes back to his car, where he joins the circle of other cabbies. Slava waves when they turn to look at her, whooping. She smudges her cigarette and the electronic doors part as she enters the airport.

She sees him, she thinks, though it's been a while and she can't be sure. He is walking with a woman and Slava's stomach drops. *Fuck*, she thinks, and considers leaving before he can see her.

It's too late, and he calls out to her. She smiles and tries to ignore the woman with him—her long black braid resting on her shoulder as she texts on her phone.

"Slava," Adam says. He continues, in Russian, "It is so good to see you—this is Dascha, I met her in the field. We had both been covering the protests in Luhansk—the protests against the protests. The pro-Russians."

The woman looks away from her phone, nods at Slava, and reaches out her hand, but Slava resists.

"You were talking to the opposition? Interviewing them? In Luhansk, you said?"

"Yes of course," says Adam. "This is a complicated political situation as you know, Slava—we must show all sides."

"You mean *your* side?" Slava decides she will send him off in a cab, let him have this other woman—Misha, perhaps, had been right.

"This is no place to have a discussion as heated as this," Dascha says. Her temperament is cool, unbothered by Slava. "We can have a conversation perhaps somewhere more private?" Turning to Adam, she asks, "Where are you staying?"

Slava waits the conversation out, eager to make an escape, but there is no resolution on a location—getting to the hotels has presented difficulty due to an army of cars—Automaidan, they called it—blocking the roads.

Slava interjects to say, "Kyiv is a labyrinth right now. Perhaps it's better we go our separate ways once we get to the city."

"Slava," Adam says, stepping near her, his breath smelling of mint gum, his hand gently squeezing her arm. "Would it be possible for us to go to your apartment?"

"All of us?" Slava asks.

"Yes," Adam says. "Dascha isn't from here, neither am I—with what we've seen of the protests we may need a base to get oriented—one that will not be overrun. Would you host us?"

Slava thinks of Maidan—*why had she ever left?*

"I will owe you," Adam says. "Please."

It's the begging that does it. That Slava realizes he's still interested, that she could be his heroine, the shepherd to the lamb.

"Yes," she said, pulling his jacket. "You will owe me."

Inside her apartment, Slava brings her guests what little food she has—some bread, cheese. She makes tea, sets it on the table.

In the living room, Dascha suggests she take the couch, and Adam agrees. Adam brings his bag to Slava's room and Slava watches him from the kitchen. Dascha asks to use the restroom, emerging fresh-faced and without makeup.

"Thank you," she says to Slava while sitting at the table. "For letting me stay."

Slava says nothing but puts a cup and a plate before her. They sit in silence until Adam emerges, dressed casually, an old American college t-shirt on.

"Are we ready to have a conversation, now?" Slava asks. Adam laughs.

"Do you want to have a conversation?" Dascha asks her. "Or do you just want a pulpit?"

"Where are you from?" Slava opens a window, the air biting cold. Her hands shake as she tries to light a cigarette. From anger, she knows—her father's hands were the same.

"Originally, I am from Crimea. But my family was pushed out. We have been living in Kharkiv, then Luhansk. I went to college in Ivano-Frankivsk. Are you from Kyiv?"

"Odesa. But I moved here when I was sixteen, seventeen."

Adam, Slava realizes, has made a place for himself leaning against the sink, nearest the door. Slava near the window, Dascha at the table. The two women stationed, the man appearing ready to flee.

Succeeding at lighting her cigarette, Slava's confidence renewed, she asks Dascha, "Did you interview friends then? In Luhansk? While you were there?"

"I did," Dascha said, the corner of her lip fighting a smile. "Is it criminal to interview friends?"

"It is criminal to support Yanukovych," Slava says. "It is treason to support Russia."

"Not everything is so black and white," Dascha says, her voice softening. Slava is disarmed by it—her sincerity. Dascha sits up, looking at her directly in the eyes. "You want a democracy—you want to be able to vote and have your voice heard. That is the nature of democracy: that not everyone will agree."

Slava says nothing, examining Dascha, her hands cupping the tea, then absent-mindedly pulling apart the bread. Neither look at Adam, who watches in silence.

"The protestors in Kyiv—your side, as you call it—they risk their lives for democracy. They risk their lives against their government, against corruption. In the east, the people in Donetsk and Luhansk—many of them have suffered since the fall of the Soviet Union. The mining, crops—the older generation tells the younger generation that under Russia, things were better. They want security, safety. The same as your side. It simply looks different to them: they see the failure of the Ukrainian government, again and again, just as you do. Their solution conflicts with yours, and that is what your side is fighting for, whether or not you realize it. You fight for the freedom to disagree. For fair elections. For a better, safer, thriving Ukraine. It's not enough to fight. When the fight is over, you will need to prove you were right. There are people who are not convinced this is right, who are older and who have seen some version of this over and over again.

"You think it's treason to speak to the other side? It's discourse. What do you want? Journalism that caters to your wants, your vision? Do you only want to know that others agree? Then you aren't looking for democracy. You are looking for another version of extremism. The other side of a flipped coin. Fascism, communism—the bigger evil depends on what you survived. Stalin was both a murderer and a hero. To ignore one reality over the other is dangerous because it is not fully the truth. We tell ourselves what we want to believe—but it is the press that must tell the truth, as ugly as it might be, so that when wars are fought, there is no propaganda. There is no soothsaying. There is only fact.

"So yes, I spoke to my friends in Luhansk, and though I disagree with them, I see their side. I share that side with you, so that maybe you will understand. So maybe this revolution will remain against evil, against the abuse of power, and I hope that it will not turn us against one another."

That night Slava lies in bed, her back to Adam, who is asleep beside her. The sex had been expected, and Slava was glad to forget.

But it was the thought of Dascha, the stranger on her couch, which troubled her. She thought of her mouth, her sardonic lip, the snakelike braid resting on her breast.

Her heartbeat slowing, Slava closes her eyes, but she does not sleep.

DEPORTATION OF THE
CRIMEAN TATARS
SUNG BY KOBZARI

I.

Before it was Ukraine, before it was Soviet Union, before it was Russian Empire, before it was Kievan Rus, Crimea was a Khanate—mixed descendants of conquerors and exiles.

The people indigenous to the peninsula were called Cumans, and later, Crimean Tatars.

Turkic language, Islamic faith.

II.

In Autumn 1941, Hitler invades Crimea. The Führer calls it *Reichskommissariat*, raises the swastika. He kills Jew, Pole, Slav, Gypsy.

Stalin crosses the sea, one side Azov, one side Black. Amphibious warfare for Soviet Christ.

By Spring 1945, Stalin takes Berlin and wins The War.

III.
Ah, ah. Fascist, Communist. Same coin, two sides.

German *Schutzstaffel*, Soviet NKVD.
Every Himmler for a Hitler.
Every Beria for a Stalin.

Beria sends a telegram, puts the Crimean Tatars in cattle trains.
One hundred-eighty thousand moved to tents, forced residences
in Uzbekistan, Kazakhstan. Soviet Tatar Soldiers, taken from
highest rank only to die in frozen labor camps.

In 1932, Stalin starved the Ukrainian. In 1944, he exiled the
Crimean Tatar.

Ukrainians call it *Holodomor*: *Death by Hunger*
Crimean Tatars call it *Sürgün*, Turkish for *Expulsion, Exile*.
Jews call it *Shoah*, Hebrew for *Destruction*.

Diaspora, Genocide: two words for saying, *Erased*.

Ah, ah—but there is Power in a name:

Israel means *Wrestles with God*.
Ukraine means *Country*

The Mongols named the peninsula, *Crimea*.
From *Qırım*, meaning, *Strength*.

ST. MICHAEL'S GOLDEN-DOMED MONASTERY
FEBRUARY 5, 2014
NIGHT

The violence on the streets outside has created a pocket of peace inside the refectory. It is late, and Katya has not gone home. She watches the Captain sleep. Misha has nodded off too—his arms crossed, sitting on the floor against a wall nearest the Captain. She feels protective over these two men. She can see the tension in both of them: the tension in their jaws, the shallow breath alighting in their chests. These men who, even in sleep, are never free. From their nightmares, their pasts, their demons.

It seems all her life, Katya has either been fighting for or against the men she loves. The room they take up in her—the staggering greed. Her child, her husband. Even her father—an elusive man Katya barely knew. It was her mother who would tell her, *It was your father who built the crib before you ever arrived.* It is the mother, though, who bleeds.

The Captain stirs in his cot, turning his head away.

It occurs to her that it's a strange miracle that she knows these two men: Misha and the Captain. If her son hadn't died, would she be here? For an instant she doesn't recognize how she got where she is, she can't recall what happened. She can't feel a thing, just shock, wonder. Perhaps fear.

In his sleep the old man whimpers and Misha shifts away from her. She remembers Ezra's back turned to her. All the nights it had been turned to her.

She doesn't want to think of him but she does. Watching the two men asleep in the belly of a church, her stomach drops. She misses Ezra. Not who he is now but who he was before. The brilliant student in medical school, head of his class. Before he was a psychiatrist, before he was her husband, he was Ezra— meeting her on the green between courses, sprawled in the grass, smoking weed.

Isn't it ridiculous, he'd say after a hard day, *that people have to suffer in the first place?*

Their first group date at a baseball game, he had lost a bet and had to wear a friend's Yankees cap and jersey. Splitting from their group and waiting in line for their beers, Katya felt a tug on her arm and a man with his friends, already wonderfully drunk, said to her: *Baby, let me take you out—you can do better than that trash.*

He lost a bet, she said, laughing. Ezra unbuttoned the jersey to reveal his real shirt underneath.

I'm undercover, Ezra said. Then, whispering to the group, *Motherfuckers won't see me coming.* He put his arm around her neck, his *Katie*, and kissed the brim of her home team cap.

The group bowled over, and the man who asked her out said to her, his breath sour, *Now that's a man of his word, and you know, you gotta respect that.*

Loyalty, the drunk man said, raising his plastic cup. *Above all.*

It was later that season that the curse broke, that they won the championship. They went into the street, the whole of New England, and confetti fell from the sky, catching in her hair, on Ezra's lip. When he kissed her she shook his hair free of it and he brushed her face, but more would land on her eyelashes, on his shoulders. They walked to her apartment, hand-in-hand, the confetti still falling, flickering in the trees, mottling the street.

They made love, and when Katya opened the shades afterward, the sky was strikingly dark.

It's these memories that are the most difficult. The ones that don't allow her to forget. The ones that suffocate. *Drown in the good times. Drink it up.*

Katya takes a breath, goes outside to smoke. When she finishes, she walks across the church grounds to the cathedral. The nurses there are working into the night. It's nearly one in the morning. She walks carefully past the injured, swaddled in blankets on the floor. She walks past the altar, toward a dressing station. A foot shoots out from under a blanket, from a patient sleeping behind a column, and Katya almost trips before she kneels, nudges it with her hands and covers it with the blanket.

She had made it home in the early morning, having just worked an overnight in the ER. She opened the bedroom door and she saw the limbs like roots peeking from the sheets, like they were anchored there. *We're not going anywhere*, their bodies seemed to say. Katya thought at first they were dead. But Ezra twisted to look up at her, and still he didn't stir. He didn't dress. He didn't apologize. Neither said a word—just held a gaze. Katya left. She learned later the woman was a colleague, a former classmate, a mutual friend.

It was her loneliness that caused her to erupt. Ezra had found a way out of his grief. She thought about them meeting, fucking, laughing. When later she had arranged to come for her belongings, it was the house that reminded her. She thought about Ezra, preoccupied with his lover, likely texting her and calling her while Katya was away, while Katya kept hearing ghosts in their home behind their son's closed bedroom door—

Isaac's toys falling on the floor. Isaac's laughter and squeals. Isaac playing games on her tablet. Isaac splashing in the bathtub. Isaac running from the monsters in the basement. Isaac crying. Isaac's heartbeat through her stethoscope.

His beat, beat, beat.

She broke the glass, the plates, the bowls. She broke the mirrors, the picture frames, the clocks. When she left the home, the floor was in shards. Katya's boots stuck with glass. She left her clothes, she left her things. She left Ezra a note: *I'll reschedule.*

She left their ghost-home and went to stay with her parents in Brookline. It was only a week later when she woke up one morning to find her mother huddled near the television, her hands knitted.

"They're beating those children, they're just beating them," her mother said, near tears. She meant the college students at Maidan, in Kyiv.

"I can help," she said. "They'll need doctors."

At first her mother pleaded with her not to go, that it was bad enough the Marathon Bombing had happened that year, that it was too soon, but it was she who helped her pack. It was her father who organized her stay at an old friend's empty apartment in Kyiv, her father who kissed her forehead before she left the car, his unexpected affection dizzying her. His cap on the seat said *Boston Strong.*

"Better take this," she said. And then she was gone.

An hour passes while Katya works in the cathedral. She takes her coat and says goodnight to the nurses who tell her to get some rest. Katya steps into the cold, and the courtyard is silent. The snow begins to fall. She closes her eyes, face upturned. She pretends for a moment that she has just left the hospital, that Ezra is waiting up for her after putting Isaac to bed. When she opens her eyes, she sees the refectory before her, and Katya, shaking herself loose from a dream, goes inside.

She finds the Captain coughing, wincing, and Misha is awake. Katya takes water to the old man, steadying the cup at his lips. Misha stays on the floor, watching her hand. She takes his vitals and checks his temperature. Something is wrong. The Captain is feverish and in pain. She asks if she can look at his wound, and he shoos her away with his able hand.

"No," he says. "No."

"It could be an infection. You have a fever."

"No," the Captain says, raising his voice. His eyes are fearful.

Katya wipes her forehead and feels inexplicably near tears. She looks away from him. She feels helpless as a child, lost. Katya says nothing. A silence passes between them.

"He doesn't want to be treated," Misha says, and Katya looks down at him as he gets up from the church floor to stand next to her.

"Captain," he says. "You need care."

Katya and Misha are silent, and the old man is looking at Katya, his eyes red and tired.

"No," he says.

Katya asks him, "Do you want to die?"

"No," the Captain says, his hand falling on hers. The ring on his finger cold as his skin.

"Yes," he says. "No."

And Katya begins to work.

SLAVA'S APARTMENT
SHOVKOVYCHNA STREET
JANUARY 23, 2014

In the morning, Dascha is gone. She left behind a note on the dining table: *Perhaps I will see you at Maidan. Thank you for a safe place to sleep.*

Slava reads the message and Adam joins her in the kitchen. He is dressed in a white dress shirt, slacks, a tie. Slava is surprised at this but quickly becomes too bored and disinterested to ask.

"Sleep well?" he asks her. Slava smiles, but he sees through it. Adam spies the note in her hand, and reads it when she puts it on the table.

"Dascha is a skilled journalist," Adam says. "She has lived a complicated life."

Slava turns toward him, aiming to chastise. "You know so much about her, then. Of course you both—"

Adam laughs at her. "No, Slava. We didn't. Dascha was not interested in me. She had a girlfriend, but they split up before she went to Luhansk. Their lives splintered."

Slava is stunned. "She told you this? Openly?"

"Yes, of course," Adam says, while rifling through the refrigerator, his tie flipped over his left shoulder.

"But depending on who she tells, where she is, it could be very dangerous for her, even here. In Russia, in parts of Ukraine."

"Well, Dascha is not someone who is unaware of the risk. She told me after she learned I was American. I mentioned my sister has a girlfriend, and we stuck close. I think you'd like her, Slava. If you give her a chance."

Slava's heart feels caught in her throat. She is flooded with memories, with her own blind terrors. Adam stops searching the fridge to ask her if she is all right, she has gone pale. He pours her a glass of water, he asks her to lie down, he leads her to the sofa, and Slava lies where Dascha had slept, breathing in.

"When I was a little girl," Slava said to Adam, without thinking, "I had a nightmare that I was gone, missing. I called for my mother and father. They must not hear me, I thought. And one day, in real life, it happened."

As if snapping back into place, Slava remembers where she is, what she is saying. She looks up at Adam, who encourages her.

"I am feeling better now," she says to him, rising. "We need to eat before we head to Maidan." She is lightheaded.

Adam urges her to lie down and she does. He tells her he must go interview representatives from Parliament, not Maidan. He tells her he is only in Ukraine for a few days before he must head to the Kremlin, where he will interview politicians there. Slava listens and studies his brown eyes as they check his watch for the time.

"You are telling me all of this now," she says to him.

"You never asked." Adam stands, goes to her room for his bag, his sport jacket.

"You are a hotshot," she says. He puts on the jacket, then his coat. "But Adam, who gives a fuck what those people think?"

"American politicians," Adam says. "Stay here, please. I will call to check in on you later. Unless you want me to call a doctor?"

Slava remembers the American doctor at St. Michael's. She thinks of Misha, who she has not heard from.

"I'm fine," Slava says. "I'll go back to sleep."

When Adam leaves, Slava closes her eyes.

ON PUNISHMENT
SUNG BY KOBZARI

Baba Yaga will eat you, Mother says when her children misbehave.
Deep in the forbidden forest, a house stilted on chicken-legs,
the lot lined by a skeleton fence, Baba Yaga makes a stew of
baby flesh.

If you don't listen, Mother says, *the police will take you away.*
Prison cell, devoid of toys—no bed, no dolls, no sunshine. No
more room to play.

I will leave you at an orphanage, Mother says, *and you'll never see
me again.*
Big brick house, plain and white. Nuns cry out, *Stay in line.*
Porridge meals. No mother, no sister, no brother, no family.

God will send the flood, says the Bishop. *He will punish you for
what you've done.*
There goes the house, there goes the village.
There goes the mother, there goes the child.
All swept up in a rising Black Sea.

Vanished, for being bad. Disappeared, for being unclean.

AUDIO CASSETTE RECORDING
SIDE ONE CONTINUED

When Stravinsky wrote *The Rite of Spring*, no one knew how to receive it. Some art is made so grotesque that despite it all you admire it—the monster outside stirring the monster within. It moves you, disquiets a part of you. And yet, eye-to-eye, each beast fully seen, laid bare.

For the Orthodox Christians in Russia and Ukraine, the believers leap into frigid waters on the January day of Epiphany. Washed clean, a shock of cold.

Le Sacre du printemps, the sacred ceremony of spring. The death of Christ. The resurrection. Ah, not for Stravinsky.

Do you know the premise? In his notes, Stravinsky said it is an episodic ballet without a cohesive beginning-to-end narrative. Instead, the episodes are bound by one unifying thread: *the mystery and great surge of the power of Spring*.

It is a violent ballet, a violent composition, taking place in pagan Russia. During the performance in 1913, the choreographer, Nijinsky, before he went mad, had the dancers move in contorted, disfigured ways. It was obscene, the audience thought—an abomination of the arts, of theatre, of ballet.

The musicians in the orchestra mocked the ballet to the point that they were told to be quiet, that there were no mistakes in the score, to just be silent and play. The conductor, Monteux, reviled the work. Yet, he performed it many times, over many years.

In Moscow, when your Aunt Anna performed the role of the Chosen One, she danced at the end, watched by the ancestors, the elders, until she dies—a sacrificial dance.

When she is at the point of exhaustion, the Ancestors run toward her. They catch her so that she does not touch the ground. They lift her up and offer her to the sky—

The night she performed in Moscow, I watched with my mother and father my sister being sacrificed.

Before she dies, a prince saves her and destroys the idol of Yarilo, the god of the sun. There is no God in Soviet Russia.

There is no one deadlier than the Kremlin. Than the State.

РЕВОЛЮЦІЯ
REVOLUTION

On the sod
In the red stains there lies
A new god.

—Sergey Gorodetsky, *Yarila*

KOZAK I
SUNG BY KOBZARI

Stretching from Middle Volga to Ryazan and Tula, to Dnieper River, free people live on the backs of horses. We call them *Kozak*: Adventurer, Freebooter, Free man.
Kozak is a Borderguard. He protects: towns, forts, settlements and trading posts.

He watches over the caravans crossing the grasslands of Ukraine. He is wild, savage, acknowledging no authority.
Beekeeper, hunter, trader, killer.

He fights the Tatars, the Poles.
He is summoned from the dead to kill Napoleon.

Sabre in hand, dressed in furs and skins, *Kozak* is a four legged-beast.
Ah, ah, but tonight: *Kozak* drives in circles across the square, packs of them protecting our barricades from Berkut.

Kozak is a Revenant burning with Hellfire.
Death Famine
War Conquest

Ah, ah. In Ukraine, we've known them all.   ·

MAIDAN NEZALEZHNOSTI
JANUARY 24, 2014

It's in the street surrounding Maidan that she sees her wearing a vest that says PRESS, dark hair long and braided, the end tied with a blue and gold ribbon. Her breath is hot, her olive cheeks are paled by the cold, and she is holding a camera.

She's interviewing a bleeding and bruised man. He is speaking about the Berkut attacks. He's part of Automaidan, a group of civilians who drive in packs to protect the protesters, and his car has been marred and crushed, and the glass shattered.

They took me, he said. *We stopped our cars. They covered our faces and took us. We thought it was a call for help, but they had lied and trapped us. Complete sabotage. We went right to them*, he said. *Others are still missing. We couldn't go to the hospital, so we went to the church.*

Dascha thanks him, and he thanks her. The sound of her voice is softer than you'd think—the way she says it, tilts her head in comfort. He tells her, *Be careful.* And she nods and says, *You too.* Dascha puts down the camera.

Slava follows, her heart a hearth, and calls after her.

Dacha looks over her shoulder, the braid falling along her back. There is Slava, her pretty mouth curiously open and her wide blue eyes and blue hair.

She says, smiling, "Hello, Slava."

"I wanted to apologize," Slava says, breathless.

"It's fine," Dascha says. "You're passionate about what you believe."

"No, please," Slava says. "I want to apologize. To have you over for dinner. Adam has gone to meet his contacts and he'll likely stay where he's been paid to stay before he goes to Moscow. Please. Tonight? Or another time?"

"Tonight, I think," Dascha says.

"Yes. Tonight."

You know the adage *Patience is a virtue.*
Love is also patient, according to Corinthians.

Slava's mother tried to show her how to learn patience. Slava's mother tried to teach her modesty, and good traditional values. She tried to teach Slava embroidery and dressmaking. Slava learned how to hold a needle, looping the thread through the eye without needing to use her tongue or her teeth. Slava's mother tried to appear good. She tried to make it all look right. She tried to love her husband, death do them part. Scarf over her long hair, Slava's mother made an offering in church and prayed. She made an offering to God. Later, she sold her daughter to the devil.

Give me patience, she'd pray. *Give me patience, Dear Lord. Let me be patient. Help me be a good wife. I pray, God. Grant me your patience, Lord.*

Slava has only once loved a woman—a girl when she was in secondary school. Marichka was her name. Marichka and Slava in her room, her mother none the wiser, thinking the two were studying or learning stitches. Until she walked in. This woman with the braid is like Marichka. Tall and fierce.

As she walks away, Slava watches Dascha on Khreshchatyk Street—a street typically for shopping. It's the main street to Maidan, and so it's barricaded and circled by the Automaidan. The street is now a village, and the people are singing and building fires. There is a stage and people are working up into a chant:

Україна це Європа!

Ukrayina tse Yevropa!

Ukraine is Europe!

Dascha holds her camera across the street with her gloved hands, recording the crowd. She turns the camera and recognizes Slava in the frame. She doesn't stop filming—she waves.

Slava takes Dascha to her apartment and the two remove their scarves and coats. Slava has made them dinner, just a simple pasta. Her mother always made the meals and Slava does now.

It's an offering: *Eat, be full.*

As they sit together, Slava listens to Dascha talk about her work as a journalist. They talk about women in the workplace, women at war, women's rights, and the female body. They talk, and they laugh.

Then, Dascha leans back in her chair and says, "You and Adam—is it serious?"

Slava looks down at her fork, her fingers lithe. The bones long and thin, the nails clipped short.

"No—I barely know him."

"He seems comfortable with you."

"People can seem to be anything. You seemed to be one way, and I was wrong."

Dascha touches the bottom of her glass, where glass meets table.

"I was wrong about you, too." They smile at one another. Slava wants to ask her about what Adam told her, but she worries she will make Dascha angry, or betray Adam.

"What about you?" Slava asks. "Is there someone in your life?"

"There was," Dascha says. "She and I ended things. It wasn't a good fit."

Slava feels herself lift—she isn't hiding from her.

"It's brave of you," Slava says, her heart beating loud, "to share that so willingly. With me."

Dascha takes a sip of her drink with a sweet grin.

"You said you protested with FEMEN—that is also very brave. I feel we have similar views, that you're accepting of me."

Slava takes a deep breath. She doesn't feel herself, or perhaps she feels for the first time she is herself. The moment terrifies her, validates her. She looks at Dascha, dark eyes bright, and feels lifted.

"I loved a girl, once," Slava said. "My mother found us, beat me bruised. She kept the secret from my father, but she said to me, 'Slava, if you keep this up, your father will certainly find out, and he will kill you.' I laughed at her and she hit me, and looked at me in a way I've never seen before—like an animal, a deer or a rabbit, trembling. And I believed what she said was true. I believed my father would kill me if he knew."

Dascha doesn't move as Slava looks up at her.

"My mother left us days later. She didn't tell me she was leaving, and I paid the price of her going. She sent a message saying to meet her, a couple days later, but she wasn't there—a man was instead. She sold me to traffickers to pay her fare. When I was free, I came to Kyiv. It took me years, but I broke free of her."

"Does your father know?"

"No," she said, the word caught in her throat.

"Do you speak to him?"

Slava thinks of her father, alone and drunk in their home in Odesa.

"Not in a while," she says. Then turning the conversation away from herself, "Do your parents know?"

Dascha smiles at Slava. "One day," she says. "I hope that yes, one day they will know all about this part of me."

Slava wants to reach for her hand, but it's Dascha who reaches first, across the table. The warmth of her palm, her lithe fingers tangled with her own, Slava's breath tightens in her chest, her eyes sting, and Dascha whispers to her, "Are you okay?"

Her whole heart open, Slava's courage renews.

AN INCOMPLETE LIST OF ANTI-PROTEST LAWS PASSED BY VERKHOVNA RADA

ON JANUARY 16, 2014

"EXTREMIST ACTIVITY" BY CITIZENS, CHURCHES, AND NONGOVERNMENTAL INSTITUTIONS IS FORBIDDEN

TRAFFIC DISRUPTION BY MOTORCADE OF MORE THAN 5 CARS
Removal of driving license and vehicle seizure up to two years

GATHERING INFORMATION OF BERKUT & JUDGES
Two years in prison

DEFAMATION BY PRESS OR SOCIAL MEDIA
One year in jail

VIOLATIONS OF RULES FOR PEACEFUL ASSEMBLIES
Identified within 24 hours

SETTING UP STAGES, TENTS, AND SOUND WITHOUT PERMISSION
Up to fifteen days in jail

PARTICIPATION IN PEACEFUL GATHERINGS WEARING A HELMET
Up to ten days in jail

GROUP VIOLATION OF PUBLIC ORDER
Up to two years in prison

BLOCKING ACCESS TO A RESIDENCE
Six years in prison

MASS DISRUPTIONS
Ten to fifteen years in prison

AUTOMAIDAN LEADER,
DMYTRO BULATOV, AGE 35

was found freezing in a ditch in the woods near Boryspil Airport. He is now receiving medical attention at Boris Clinic.

Bulatov had led a motorcade of 2,000 vehicles to the home of Ukrainian President Victor Yanukovych on December 29th. On January 23, around 4 a.m., the Berkut arrested fifteen Automaidan activists outside Hospital No. Seventeen.

Until today, this was the last time Bulatov had been seen.

Badly bloodied and scarred, Bulatov's ear had been cut off and he had piercings in his nails—evidence of crucifixion. Police attempted to arrest Bulatov for mass disorder—a violation of Anti-Protest Laws. However, the medical staff created a blockade encircling Bulatov and the hospital, protecting him from police.

The government opposition warns of Death Squads:
Think *Einsatzgruppen.*
Think *Cheka.*
Think *NKVD.*
All return to Ukraine.

THE RITUAL OF ABDUCTION

He met her a few blocks from her home, took her in a car, promised her she would be reunited with her mother.

Where are we going? she said to him. *Where is Mama?* She did not raise her voice. She did not want to show him she was afraid.

He took her to an apartment and there were other women there. They did not wear clothes and the women were smudged and dirty. The women there looked tired, smoking. They looked at Slava and they did not look at Slava. There were men there too, fucking some of the women. Other women and men were watching. Tired eyes, all of them. The women with bruises on them. Some people Slava couldn't tell who they were—women or men.

I heard you are a whore, he said. He said, *I heard from your mother you like to fuck women and men.*

He pointed at a girl and she came over. She had makeup on that had dirtied her face. The lipstick had puffed her mouth and reddened her chin. She faced Slava but she did not look at her. Slava remembers how she looked through her, as if she didn't see her. Slava understood and tried to look through her, too. She didn't know how.

Undress her, he said. The ghost woman went for Slava's shirt and Slava slapped her hands away. The woman tried again, and Slava pushed her. The woman did not fight her. She kept trying, robotically, to take the clothes off of Slava and Slava deflected.

He got impatient. He pushed the woman away and ripped off Slava's shirt and she cried.

Fuck her, he said. *Fuck her. I want to see you.*

No. No.

The ghost woman came up close to her and whispered into her ear:

это скоро закончится

Eto skoro zakonchitsya

Soon it will be over.

She said, undressing her, *Don't let them know you are afraid.*

ST. MICHAEL'S GOLDEN-DOMED MONASTERY
FEBRUARY 7, 2014
EVENING

The old man wakes but Katya has gone. Mikhail Tkachenko is in the chair beside him, barely awake. Their eyes meet briefly, neither saying a word. The old man feels hungry. The pain he feels in his body has awoken him, kept him awake, but he knows it will not keep him awake for long.

The holy men have begun singing again, and a priest prays over an ailing woman down the hall. People are on the floor, lying on blankets, lying on backpacks, on coats.

Misha, sitting beside him, closes his eyes, listening. The Captain hums, matching the key. Like tea in his throat—the melody warm and smooth.

SLAVA'S APARTMENT
SHOVKOVYCHNA STREET

It goes like this for weeks, into mid-February—Slava and Dascha meet at Maidan and enter the apartment at the threshold. They make love, make dinner, make love. Sometimes the camera on, sometimes the camera off.

"I think I would like to paint you," Slava says to Dascha one night.

Slava has a number of pictures in her apartment bedroom, her beautiful friends from FEMEN who posed outside, bare-breasted, fake blood and paint on their bodies, phrases like "FUCK PUTIN" on their bellies, wreaths of flowers on the crowns of their heads, ribbons falling down their backs.

"Let me paint you," Slava says. "Please."

Dascha focuses the camera on Slava's light eyes. She has started filming their time together, at Maidan and at the apartment.

"One day," Dascha says, "I promise."

ALEKSANDR IVANOVICH, BROTHER OF BELOVED SOLOIST BALLERINA, ANASTASYA IVANOVA, MARRIES NEDEZDHA VASILIEVA

Aleksandr Arkadyevich Ivanovich, brother of famed Bolshoi soloist ballerina, Anna Arkadyevna Ivanova, married Nedezdha Stepaneva Vasilieva, age twenty, also a soloist, at Leningrad Marriage Palace on May 26, 1966.

The two met at an afterparty following the Bolshoi Ballet premiere of *The Rite of Spring* in Moscow, 1965, where Miss Ivanova performed the role of the Chosen One, the sacrificial virgin who is avenged by her lover.

"I don't want to take all the credit," Miss Arkadyevna Ivanova said about the couple, laughing. "I suppose Sasha could also thank Mr. Stravinsky."

Miss Ivanova and the new Mrs. Ivanova will be performing with the Bolshoi Ballet in Cuba later this year. Cuban President Osvaldo Dorticós Torrado and Prime Minister Fidel Castro are said to be in attendance.

Miss Stepaneva Vasilieva and Mr. Arkadyevich Ivanovich exchanged their vows among family and friends, toasting champagne and dancing into the night. A truly romantic and joyful evening was punctuated by the words of council member, Elena Svetlana Antonina: "I wish you happiness and love. Complete happiness is impossible without complete labor for your country!"

TRADE UNIONS BUILDING BOMBED
FEBRUARY 6, 2014

The Trade Unions Building—
the headquarters for anti-government protestors
a press center, security center,
a kitchen—

received a package labeled with the word:
Medicine.

It sounded like a heartbeat in our hands:

Tick
Tick
Tick

Ka-Boom.

SLAVA'S APARTMENT
SHOVKOVYCHNA STREET
FEBRUARY 8, 2014

In the morning, to avoid the neighbors, Dascha leaves quietly before the sun rises, and Slava, heavy with languor, lies in bed until the afternoon, when she goes to Maidan to hand out gloves, soup, tea. She sings songs, helps carry stone and bricks. She shovels the snow, she helps the men find what they need, whatever they need. The protests continue on Hrushevsky Street, just a few blocks from Slava's apartment, and she can walk home when it gets late.

The protest lives on, and Slava wears a helmet. Invigorated by love, she ties ribbons in the holes of the Berkut shields and tells them, "Brothers, join us." Slava feels like an angel, like a saint. She goes home with Dascha—her heart swelling like the moon.

One morning, Slava's phone buzzes with a text.

Dascha turns in bed and sees the phone light up and wakes Slava. "Is it Misha? Is he okay?" Dascha asks.

Slava is touched. She opens her phone without lifting her head from her pillow.

"Adam," Slava says. "He is in Moscow but might come back to Ukraine."

"Are you going to meet him?" Dascha asks her, and Slava sighs in the dark.

"I don't know," she says. "God, he will be heartbroken!"

Dascha laughs, and Slava searches her lover's body. The valley between the breasts, the crater of the belly button, the ravine of the female sex. She wants again to paint her, to cover her in paint, to paint her likeness, to document her, every inch, freckle, blemish.

"Come to me," Slava says, kissing her, and her lover hums. "Dascha, come."

PHRASES ON EUROMAIDAN PROTEST POSTERS

THE NATION IS INVINCIBLE

I AM UKRAINIAN AND I CAN'T KEEP CALM

PUTIN IF YOU LOVE US—LET US GO

FUCK YANUKOVYCH

STOP PUTIN STOP WAR

UKRAINE IS EUROPE

YANUKOVYCH IS NOT UKRAINE

NO PUTIN NO KILLING

VICTORY WILL BE OURS

POLICE WITH THE PEOPLE

ONLY A COWARD WOULD HURT A CHILD

WE DO NOT WANT WAR

RUSSIA, HANDS OFF UKRAINE

NO VIOLENCE AT EUROMAIDAN

UKRAINE IS MY CHILD

I BREATHE FREELY

AGAINST THE POLICE STATE

SHAME IN FRONT OF THE WORLD

I AM A DROP IN THE OCEAN

PAVLYCHENKO APARTMENT
FEBRUARY 8, 2014

There were two things that kept Misha alive after Vera died:

The first was his mother, who would say to him, "I've out-lived my husband, my daughter-in-law, my friends, some of their children. I've lost my home, I've lost everything but you, my son." Then she would kiss his forehead, his hands. She prayed he would leave the mines in Donetsk every night before she went to bed, every morning when she woke up, the blood-colored rosary in her soft, thin hands.

The second were his friends Petro and Nadia Pavlychenko, who hosted him for weekly dinners after Vera died.

Petro has called him this morning to invite Misha over.

"Bring a friend," Petro had said. "Or are we your only ones?"

"The girls will be happy to see you, Misha," Nadia said on the speakerphone. "What has it been? Four months?"

"Yes, I know," Misha replied. "Back before this all started."

"Can you believe it, Misha?" Petro added. "Last time I saw you, we were watching Dynamo murder Lutsk. Remember that game? Now, we watch our police murder our neighbors."

"Yes," said Misha. "It seems impossible."

"Bring someone," said Nadia. "Bring a date."

He didn't plan to ask her, at first. It would be easiest and cleanest to keep their only interaction at the church. He could admire her there, and when she'd have to leave Kyiv, the monastery would be his only memory of her.

It was only after he heard her laugh at a joke he'd made, while they stood smoking outside the refectory that afternoon. It was such an unexpected and beautiful sound that he forgot what he had said to cause it, and they laughed together, the sun almost warm, the moment a miracle.

"Katya," he asked her, emboldened, "I wonder if you'd like to have dinner with me and my friends. They're the dearest people I know."

She didn't answer at once, and he worried he'd made a mistake until she said, "I would love to, Misha. Yes."

During the Orange Revolution, Vera and Misha met Nadia and Petro. It was their first year in Kyiv. At the protests, they held hands and sang together. Vera had braided her own hair like Yulia Tymoshenko, a wreath of braids pinned around her head like a crown. Petro and Nadia were a young couple with little twin girls—an ideal family. Misha talked with Petro on the balcony and Vera played games with the girls. Nadia had tied orange ribbons in their hair. Misha learned to braid by practicing with the children.

When Misha reflects on this memory, he recalls how Vera was healthy and beautiful. They had been married a year and were trying for a child. Both girls were in love with his young, happy wife, sitting on her lap, showing her their dolls, showing her their shoes and dresses, complimenting her eyes, asking their mother for ribbon to make Vera bracelets to wear at the protest.

Oh Misha, Vera would say, *I love those girls.*

Vera wanted a girl, Misha doesn't tell Katya as they walk from the monastery. *She wanted to name her after Nadia. We thought we couldn't have children, both of us being children of Chernobyl.*

It broke Vera's heart, he doesn't say.

Misha and Katya walk toward the outskirts of Kyiv, away from the barricades, and it's quiet. After the noises of Maidan and the cacophony inside the church, the quiet feels foreign to them both. The sound of peace. They do not disturb it.

Little has changed with the Pavlychenko family over the years except age. The twins, Olena and Nina, have grown to be young women, fourteen years old, and Nadia and Petro, have grown some gray strands like Misha.

"You must be Katya," Nadia says, and hugs her. Nadia looks at Misha over Katya's shoulder and winks. Olena compliments Katya's boots, asks if she can take her coat.

Nina watches them all, a cool grin on her pink face, and says, "We're so happy you're here."

At dinner, Petro, his face round and nose red, says, "I went to the Maidan only a few times. It was in the beginning, before the Berkut came. I was curious, nostalgic. The girls wanted to go. So, I took them. Nadia painted their faces, we put ribbons in their hair. We went again during the March of Millions when things, we thought, were safer. When it became too violent, we stopped going, but the girls went out a couple of times with friends, they volunteered to hand out supplies and food. I tried to keep them from going, but Nadia said, 'It's their future, Petro,' and I knew she was right. Our parents didn't want us to go during the Orange Revolution, but we did—we went for the girls. Now, they could go for themselves."

The girls look at one another and smile, radiant. Katya asks the girls about their studies, and Nadia, sitting next to Misha, leans into his elbow.

"How did you meet?" she whispers.

"*Mykhaylivs'kyi*," he says, lifting his fork.

"I don't see a ring,"

"She's not wearing one," he says.

"She's wonderful, Misha," Nadia says.

"She is. She's married," Misha says.

"An affair then, Misha?"

"No. A friendship."

"Surely, her marriage is over."

"Nothing is ever sure until you're dead."

"You haven't changed a day," Nadia whispers, laughing.

When it is time for Misha and Katya to leave, Nadia and Petro take Misha aside as Katya says goodbye to the girls.

"Doesn't it feel like we're caught in some kind of loop, Misha?" Petro asks him.

"It feels that way."

"It's good to see you, Misha," Nadia says. "Please come over again. It felt like old times, like good times."

Misha nods. He wonders if times are ever good or bad, or whether it's simply the people who make them that way. And if tonight felt like old times, like good times, what does it mean that Vera is not here?

Petro looks over at Katya, his daughters. Misha looks, too.

"Vera would have liked her," he says to Misha.

"I know," Misha says, and Petro grabs him fraternally at the the nape of his neck. He holds his hand there for a moment, as if grounding him. When his hand lifts, Misha feels himself unmoored.

It's the first time his friends said her name tonight. It seems as if it should hurt, it seems like it should be an insult or a swear, but instead it feels like a fact. A declaration. The wall is red. The cat is asleep. Vera isn't here. Vera is gone. Vera is dead.

When Katya is ready to leave, Misha holds the door. And so, they go.

"Back to our dear Captain," she says when they are back outside, wrapping her neck with her scarf.

Surely, her marriage is over.

Surely, my wife is dead.

Surely, this woman likes me.

She has no idea. This woman has no idea who I am.

"I was thinking—my apartment is nearby. Instead of going to the church, I could make us some tea. I haven't checked on the place in a week. It's just a couple blocks away."

A silence as Katya considers. Only the sound of boots on snow, on wet pavement. Misha finds his heart is in his throat, and he's not sure why he's so afraid.

"I would like to see your home," Katya says to him.

MISHA'S APARTMENT
FEBRUARY 8–9, 2014

He asks her if she'd like tea, coffee.

"Tea, please," she says.

"I'm sorry for the mess."

"It's nice."

There is little in the apartment. There's a bed, a stove, a chair, a table. A small television, a door, and a balcony. Katya sits in the chair, a heavy, dark green fabric. The cushion worn so that she sinks into it. Her arms on either side, as if she were sitting on a throne.

Misha goes to the stove and lights the burner, a flint of blue. He looks at her, a flint of blue.

I have a husband, she thinks. *I used to have a son.*

"Is it difficult being here?" Misha asks her, filling the kettle. "Do you miss home?"

"I hardly think of home when there's so much to do here."

"It's never too busy to think of home," Misha says. "Do you miss Boston?"

"Yes, I do miss Boston. Do you miss home? Donetsk?"

"I don't know if Donetsk is home. Or if Kyiv is home. In some ways Dnipropetrovsk is home—I was married there, went to university there."

"I didn't know you were married."

"I was. She passed away."

"I'm sorry."

"No need. It was a long time ago."

"We grew up in Pripyat. My father was an engineer at Chernobyl. He and my wife died from the same disease, years apart. Perhaps Pripyat, truly, is home. "

"I'm sorry, Misha."

"Nadia and Petro knew her. Loved her. They liked you. She would have liked you, too."

The kettle begins to sing. Misha turns to pour the tea. He sits beside her, placing two mugs.

"I had a son," Katya says, as he settles. "He was six."

Misha looks at her, steady.

"Heart failure. Well, that was the root of it. It was a quiet illness—something that appeared at first as trouble breathing, a fever, chest pain, a rash. Ezra—that's my husband—we took him to the hospital and the doctors there told us that it was pump failure. The cause was rheumatic fever—A *Streptococcus*. Strep throat—something easily treatable. Or, should have been."

"I'm sorry," Misha says.

"Please," she says. "Nothing to be sorry for." She cups her hand over the tea. Warm, hot, like breath.

"When Isaac died," she says, "I felt I couldn't go anywhere. Everywhere was a memory. The kitchen, the bedroom, his room—everything was, 'this is where Isaac used to take a bath,' and 'this is where he built the tower with all the pillows with Ezra,' and 'this is where he ate breakfast.' Everything becomes this reminder—this mirror you can't look away from—where you see what you've lost.

"I used to wander around the house looking for him. I would wake up from sleep, thinking I heard him crying, and Ezra would find me in the kitchen, in the living room. I'd wake up and want to break everything in the house. Once, I did. I drank, and I barely drank before. But I would come home from the hospital after days and days of being on my feet and I wouldn't move during the time I had off. I would stare at the wall. Ezra would find me there. He shut down. Looked away.

"He found me in the kitchen, one night, drunk. I threw all our glasses at him, telling him I wanted to hurt him. I wanted him to feel something. The kitchen was layered in broken glass, and he had to carry me out of the room to keep me from cutting myself. He took me to a hospital. I started counseling, started taking medication. We never said a word about it to one another. I was getting better, I knew. I wrote in a journal. I started going deeper. I started healing. Ezra told me he had started seeing a therapist, too. I thought we were healing together. The bombing in Boston last year, I thought, brought us closer. But one day, I came home from work early from a shift—I had a canceled surgery—and I found Ezra in bed with her. The therapist."

Katya picks up the mug and looks at Misha. His gaze steadies her. *This man is a boulder*, she thinks. *Not a rock: a boulder. A mountain.*

"I wasn't even angry—just in shock. I couldn't feel. Ezra didn't apologize. He sat at the edge of the bed and looked at me. We just stared at one another, and the woman didn't move. We all waited there—I don't know how long—and Ezra got up and said he would go, and I told him, no. I said, I'll go. And they left the room and let me pack."

Misha puts down his glass. He leans over the table that separates them.

"What will you do when this finally ends?" he asks. His eyes a mirror. "Because it must end some time."

"I don't know," she says. "I haven't spoken to him. I knew I couldn't stay there: I realized it then. I couldn't stay in that house with my son's ghost and my dead marriage. It was as if the whole world opened up before me, splitting like a grapefruit, saying, *Go.*

"I heard of the protests in Ukraine from my mother, that there were doctors from all around that were volunteering to help. I gave my hospital notice for a leave of absence. I told Ezra and I was gone in a week."

Misha doesn't speak for some time. Katya brings the tea to her lips. It's hot, still, and it burns her tongue.

"After the explosion," Misha says, "they evacuated Pripyat. We moved to Dnipropetrovsk, where I finished grade school and college. I was eleven when it all happened. Vera and her mother moved with us, and my father helped find an apartment for them—not long before he started getting sick. Vera's mother always enjoyed drinking, especially wine—she and my mother loved to get together when we were little and the men were out. After the disaster, she didn't stop."

"You were there then? At Chernobyl? Both you and Vera?"

Misha nods. "Yes," he says.

Katya doesn't say anything. But he knows what she thinks. She's too polite to ask, *what was it like?*

How much energy does it take to remember?

"Vera tried to stay out of the house. She hadn't gone to the conservatory right away—she worked at a restaurant after school and she liked that. She liked the busy-ness of it, pleasing people, making small talk and asking after their families. Everyone loved her. But she had a dark side. Only I saw it.

"I had gone to Donetsk twice in my life. The first was after college for work—I was hired as an engineer. A good job, I thought.

"Vera was upset when I moved away—she thought I didn't love her. She told me she went to a bar that night with her friends from college, and a man asked her out. She said she would go out with him if I didn't come home. I told her I couldn't come home. I told her I couldn't, I had just started. I told her she needed to do what she needed to do. She hung up on me.

"When I came home, a couple weeks later on a break, I went by her house and she wasn't there. Her mother answered the door and invited me inside, but I went away. I went down to the bar myself and had a drink. I waited.

"She came by the bar. I asked her if she went out with the guy she met, and she nodded. I felt sick and sad. She started sobbing. I just walked away and started down the street. She called after me. When I saw her again, standing there, ruptured as a rainstorm, a downpour on her face, I asked her to marry me. She said yes.

"I knew I had been foolish. I had loved her all my life. We were survivors of Chernobyl—children of a different nation. All our lives we had been outsiders, but we had been outsiders together.

"So, she took care of her mother, worked at the restaurant, and I would come once a month to Dnipropetrovsk. We got married. We came to Kyiv after her mother died, hoping for a fresh start. That was the summer before the Orange Revolution. But then I went back to Donetsk because we needed more money— I was here less. I wasn't there when Vera was diagnosed, not right away. I was making trips again. My mother stayed here and took care of her because it became harder for me to leave the mines. The medical bills, the people I worked for—"

Misha remembers the cassettes delivered each week with his wife's voice, how he waited for them, how he'd listen to them over and over until a new set arrived. He would listen to the sound of her playing the piano as he bent over the engineering plans, as he drove to the illegal and legal mines, sometimes even as he took the elevator cage down. How surely Misha had wanted to leave Donetsk, to abandon the path he had started on.

"You know, when the plant blew up, I thought that was the worst of it. A terrible tragedy that affected our community—but we'd rebuild. It wasn't like that. The disease of it was in our

110

bodies, in the land, in the air. It didn't just kill the people I loved, it festered inside of them. It grew. I wasn't even sure what it meant, still, when I was a kid and I found out my dog was sick, my dad was sick. I thought, 'When you get sick, you get better.' But my dog didn't get better, and neither did my dad. And then years later, Vera became sick.

"I didn't think people could live there anymore, but I heard stories about some old women whose husbands died, the *samosely*. I tried to convince my mother not to return. She said that it was the only place she ever felt at home. A couple hundred *babushkas* had returned and she went with them. Women in their seventies, eighties having survived Stalin, genocide. My mother was the youngest of them when she went back, after Vera passed—she was in her sixties. She said that's where she wants to die. Who am I to tell her no?

"It sounds crazy, but when I was kid, I worried about everything my mother ate and drank after my father died. I imagined the water was poison, the food was poison, and it probably all was, but I was afraid I would wake up one day and she'd be asleep still, and she wouldn't wake up.

"Now, she and the *babushkas* farm the land, she works day in, day out. She looks the best she has ever looked. She's stronger than she's ever been. I don't worry for her anymore. Now she just worries for me."

Misha stops.

"I haven't told anyone that," he says. "At least not all of it."

Katya pulls her knees into her chest, her socked feet on the chair. Both look at the table, the cups of tea.

"Neither have I," she says.

Reaching out for her, he takes her hand. She feels her own heart in her throat, in her ears, in her chest. As a doctor she feels touch often, but this is different. She feels the warmth of touch, the kind of touch that circles back. The kind of touch made hungry, the kind of touch that fills.

Katya doesn't remember the last time she's been touched.

She wants, without thinking, *More.*

She watches her hand, like a bird in his palm, as he traces the fine bones of her wrist. She leans into him. She can feel his breath on her, they're so close.

He wants to kiss her palm, the crook inside her elbow, the shallow of her clavicle. He holds her hand and the wedding ring is gone, and he wants to swallow her finger whole. He feels himself rise, the energy of God, the energy of fruit. He wants to lick her palm and taste her heat. He wants to keep her warm, keep her here.

Ah, ah—my friend:
What do we do when the world ends?
What do we do when the war begins?
What do we do, buried in a bunker?
We love.

UKRAINIAN JOURNALIST
ASSAULTED, BEATEN
DECEMBER 25, 2013

Tetiana Chornovol—journalist, wife, and mother—was driving home from Maidan near Boryspil Airport, followed by two cars. Hours before, Tetiana had published an article exposing corruption within the Ukrainian Minister of Internal Affairs.

A Porsche Cayenne rammed her off the road. Two men dragged her onto the asphalt, beat her, threw her in a roadside ditch, left her for dead.

She should have been dead, the way she looked—face puffed and red, red the color of her sweater, her lips purple-bruised so she couldn't speak. One eye closed shut, the nose draining blood down her cheek.

Tetiana lies on the white sheet of a hospital bed, her black hair tucked under her battered head. At Maidan, we carry photos of her disfigured face into the street.

Meanwhile, the number of missing journalists and protestors continues to grow.

SLAVA'S APARTMENT
SHOVKOVYCHNA STREET
FEBRUARY 17–18, 2014

"Take off your clothes," Slava says, picking up a pencil, heavy paper.

"Just like the *Titanic*," Dascha says, lifting her shirt over her head.

She has a bruise on her ribs, on her left thigh from Maidan. Slava has kissed them profusely, but they refuse to heal.

"Heal," she whispered into the bruises. "Heal."

"Now," she says to Dascha, "untie your hair."

Dascha pulls her dark hair free, and it's kinked from the braid.

"I'll sketch first," Slava says, "to practice. And next time, we'll paint."

Slava draws the bend of her lover's forehead, the drape of her hair, the fur of her sex, the rough follicles of her unshaven calves. She meditates on her bruises, dark and heavy like her areolae, and the scar from her youth across the knee. When she finishes, she kisses the portrait, and Dascha laughs. Then, she kisses her lover, lies beside her, and draws her with her mouth.

When they finish, Dascha says to her, "I thought you would paint me—like the other women."

Slava, joyful and surprised, turns to her. "Now?"

"Yes. And I want to dye my hair," Dascha says. "A color like yours."

Slava takes a lock of Dascha's dark hair and says, "We'll have to bleach it."

In her apartment, Slava keeps dyes of every color, so she can change her mind. Purple, green, blue, pink, red. She takes out the boxes to show Dascha.

"Pink," Dascha says.

Dascha sits in a chair in the kitchen, a towel wrapped around her. Slava brushes her hair, pulls it back from the scalp, and, wearing gloves, fills her palm with the lightening bleach.

"Are you sure?" she asks, and Dascha nods, saying, "Yes."

"Okay," Slava says. She combs the bleach through her lover's thick hair.

"It might burn," she says, and Slava dabs her fingers along the fine hairs of Dascha's scalp.

Dascha's eyes water but she asks Slava, "How does it look?"

Slava takes off her gloves, starts making them cups of coffee. "I think you might love it," she says. They sit together at the kitchen table with coffee and wait.

Slava watches Dascha write on her laptop. No matter how tired she returns from Maidan, Dascha makes love to Slava, and then she reviews the footage she's shot, and she writes long after Slava has fallen asleep. Slava is fascinated by her devotion, by the ritual of it.

Slava asks her, "Why did you become a journalist here? When you know it's so dangerous? You can go anywhere. You can make more money."

Dascha keeps working, doesn't look up. She says, "Why did you join FEMEN? It's the same."

"FEMEN left," Slava says. "You're here. You stayed. I want to hear you tell it."

"I am a filmmaker," Dascha says. "I am a lesbian filmmaker—a Ukrainian? A Crimean? A Russian? I am not the only one who feels this way. You can see it—at Maidan. People are willing to die in protest for their beliefs. For a better life. Today, we fight against Putin. Tomorrow, we fight against hate.

"This won't be over for a long time, Slava. Something is coming. I have a colleague who wants to meet because it's too dangerous to write in an email. The Kremlin's reach is wide. But we have to fight, Slava. You didn't go to France. You stayed because there is more that needs to be done, personal safety be damned. I stay and work because I have to believe there is a reason worth staying. Not just Ukraine's story—but my story. Your story. Our story. I do this because I believe in us—all of Ukraine."

While Dascha is in the shower rinsing the bleach, Slava takes out a box of paint, and a box of wreaths. She chooses a wreath with faux blue and gold flowers, one of the last she made. She takes ribbons from the box and cuts them long, tying them at the back of the wreath, like a train on a veil.

She thinks about the women in FEMEN, the ones she knows in France. She remembers, without a pang of guilt, of her decision to stay.

Slava has a faint smile on her lips as Dascha returns to the bedroom, her hair a yellow-blond, burned in parts with orange. Her lover looks shy, but her eyes are bright from the sex, the bleach, the blond.

"It worked," Dascha says, and she puts on her underwear, lounge pants. She leaves her chest bare, and Slava motions for her to sit in a chair across from her.

She chooses golden yellow, blue, and black. She dabs the brush in blue, and the cold paint causes Dascha to shiver. Slava paints across the clavicle, shoulder to shoulder, the breasts and the sternum. In yellow, she paints over a mole on Dascha's belly, the tender bruise on her ribs, causing Dascha to close her eyes. On the Ukrainian flag, she paints in black the word, *slava*—Ukrainian for *glory*.

"And now it dries," she says, and Dascha follows her into the kitchen, where they trim the dead ends of her blond hair and dye it pink.

She watches Dascha, leaning over the sink in the kitchen, her hair rinsing, turning the stream a carnation. Slava sweeps, pulling up tufts of Dascha's blond hair brushed from the tile. Dascha dries her soaking hair with a towel, the pink strands framing her face. Her hair is shorter, now only to her shoulders. Seeing Slava watching her, Dascha smiles. The rest of the night, Dascha wears the *kalyna* crown.

Slava finds a note in the kitchen, the same place she has always left it, saying Dascha has gone to Maidan. Slava looks at her phone and there are messages from Adam and Misha.

The text from Adam: *I saw the news, are you okay?*

The text from Misha: *Avoid HQ. Huge fire.*

Both: *Text when you see this so I know you're safe.*

Slava dresses, readies herself to go to Maidan. She feels her stomach knot, and she sits on the bed, summoning courage. Then she sees the pillowcase, the prints Dascha's hair has made, the stain like a watercolor in the fabric, blossoming.

The ends faded but reaching, staining fiber by fiber, like blood.

IGOR STRAVINSKY
ON MEMORY

My earliest memory is of the sound of the ice breaking on the River Neva in St. Petersburg near where I was born. It was the sound that marked the beginning of a new year, a new spring.

My other memory is of the church.

But perhaps the strongest memory of my childhood is of the country fairs I was taken to in the Ukraine. The songs which I heard and the dances which I saw have stayed in my imagination all my whole life.

EXTERMINATION OF THE
KOBZARI BY STALIN
SUNG BY KOBZARI

We were asked by Stalin to come to a Congress of Folk Singers in Moscow—all the *kobzari* in Ukraine, together.
Many of us blind, we found one another, each from small villages, as guides helped us find our way to the train car.

We carried within our bodies vibrations of all *kobzari* before us—songs that were sang to us that we learned to sing. While the government burned our books, we continued to sing.

No written lyric, no written note—
Each song a memory, each song a revolution.

Stalin said, *Let life be better, let life be merrier. Come to Moscow, let us build a unified future!*

And so we traveled to the congress *for Kobzari, Lirniki* and *Banduristy.* We brought the bandura, we brought melody, we brought with us memory.

We sang in the train car, joyfully we played—all of us far from home, all of us together. We sang until the car stopped in the dead of night.

The trenches had been dug before we had arrived.
The NKVD soldiers led us and our guides to the edge, the soil slipping beneath our feet.
They shot us in the dark and covered us in earth and lime.

Let this song be an excavation. Let this hallowed ground be known.

ГРУШЕВСЬКОГО
HRUSHEVSKY

*You become more interested in death
when you bury friends.*

—Serhiy Zhadan

PROTESTORS MASSACRED BY BERKUT PARAMILITARY POLICE FORCE

FEBRUARY 19, 2014

ADAM VOADEN, EASTERN EUROPE CORRESPONDENT

More deaths were reported on Tuesday, February 18, on the streets of Kyiv. Protestors have been gathering in the city center, Independence Square, since November of last year. Approximately 20,000 protestors marched Tuesday morning on Verkhovna Rada, the Ukrainian Parliament.

Police began to attack protestors with stun grenades around 10:00 on Shovkovychna and Lypska Streets, and by 11:00 witnesses reported snipers shooting on demonstrators. Video footage and photographs of the scene showed the police armed with AK-74 assault rifles near the Party of Regions on Lypska Street. Demonstrators attempted to ward off the police with Molotov cocktails, bricks, and other projectiles.

At 17:04, protestors were caught off-guard by a Berkut assault. As protestors surveyed a drone hovering near the area, the police ambushed the crowd from the rear by penetrating a barricade on

Hrushevsky Street near Dynamo Stadium. The police threw grenades and shot civilians as they fled down Khreshchatyk Street toward Maidan, where demonstrators stacked burning debris to fortify a wall protecting them from the police forces.

The death toll by the end of the early morning of February 19 was estimated at 28, including 10 police deaths.

After attempts for peace-keeping negotiations with President Yanukovych failed, it is estimated that another 70–100 protestors have been fatally shot by the police force, with medical and forensic services working to identify the bodies.

SHOVKOVYCHNA STREET
FEBRUARY 18, 2014
MORNING

Misha receives a text message back from Slava: *There is a march outside my apartment this morning. Will you be there?*

Misha takes his construction helmet, painted with the Ukrainian flag—Slava made the design—and his shield, stolen from a Berkut, and makes his way to Shovkovychna Street.

I'll meet you outside, he texts back.

Misha sees her, wearing a green coat, blue hair trailing from under a beanie. She smiles at him as he walks up to her, but the sound of gunfire makes her duck, makes her cry out, and Misha covers her with the shield.

The protesters, hands in the air, are saying to the police who shoot them, "Defend your people! Defend your people! Stand with us!" Some men and women lie in the street. Some men are dressed from Maidan, wearing makeshift military gear, but mostly people are wearing suits and dresses—people who, while on their way to work decided to stop, decided to peacefully march.

The people cry, pleading for mercy on Hrushevsky Street. The Berkut police hear the people cry, and they shoot until the crying stops.

Slava and Misha don't want to die, so they run. Misha is struck by a Berkut dressed in black, by his iron baton. Misha falls to the pavement, the Berkut goes for Slava.

Two large protestors wearing balaclavas see the Berkut and go after him. The Berkut swings at them, pushes them back with his metal shield. The protestors overcome the Berkut, taking away his baton, beating him with it. They take the shield. They beat the Berkut man until he stops moving.

Misha yells at them to stop. Slava is crying, shaking. Both screaming at the men to stop, stop.

Bang. Bang. The men run off. One of them falls next to the Berkut. Slava is crying, and she holds onto Misha's hand.

"Let's go," she says. "Come, Misha."

Slava leads Misha to St. Michael's.

ST. MICHAEL'S GOLDEN-DOMED MONASTERY
FEBRUARY 18, 2014
LATE MORNING

All of Maidan is there. The church and the monastery are made into a full hospital. When Slava and Misha enter, they see bodies covered in white sheets. Slava looks away.

Katya is there. Slava remembers the pretty doctor and she calls out to her. Katya sees her, sees Misha, and leads them to a spot beside the Captain. Misha sits on the floor on a sleeping bag, and a medic brings him a blanket. Katya kneels beside him, begins to examine the wounds on his shoulder.

"Slava," he says, head aching, "this is Katya." When she spies the doctor shake her head at him, a tired smile, Slava knows they are in love.

She watches the doctor as she works, asking Misha where the pain is, and as he guides her, Slava watches the doctor's moves, following his voice like a map. She, a cartographer of the body, tells him she needs him to take off his coat. Slava steps aside. She takes her phone out and calls Dascha, but there is no answer. Just Dascha's recorded voice.

Dascha says, *Zalyshte meni povidomlennya—*
Leave me a message—

After the doctor finishes inspecting Misha, Slava asks her, "Will he be okay?"

"We will check for broken ribs," Katya says. "I will see if we can run the X-rays here. As a last result he will need to go to the hospital."

Turning to Slava, Katya asks, "Are you okay? Have you been hurt?"

"No, I am okay," Slava says, shaking. "I have to go. I need to find someone."

"You should stay, Slava," Katya says, worried. "It's not safe. Please."

Slava is trembling and she feels as if she can't breathe. Everything feels shallow and heavy and like it's moving too fast. She feels her heart beating in her throat, and she feels hot and cold at once. She sees the doctors and the medics and the hurt people in Kyiv and she combs her fingers through her fine hair and tries to breathe, but it feels as if she's drowning in the church, under water, under snow, submerged beneath all that pain.

"I have to find her," Slava says, dizzy with fear. "I love her and she could be dead."

The doctor leads her away to a corner, asks her to sit. It's still loud, fast, but Slava can lean her head against the church wall. Katya brings her a blanket, a water bottle, and a blister pack of ten pills.

"Here. These are point two five milligrams of alprazolam. I want you to take one now and hold on to the rest."

Slava takes the pill. She feels herself slow. After a few minutes, Katya returns, kneels next to her. The doctor looks tired, her hair pulled back, strings of it loose around her temples, a medical mask around her neck.

"When you feel better, and if you decide to leave," Katya gives Slava a slip of paper with her phone number, "put this into your phone and text me so I can reach you. If I don't hear back from you in a couple hours, if you don't call, I'm going to worry."

"Okay," Slava says.

"What is her name just in case she comes this way?"

"Dascha Bandura. She's twenty-seven. She's a journalist. Tall, pink hair."

"Okay," Katya says. "We will do our best."

"Thank you," Slava says. She rises. She walks past the bodies, the immobile white sheets, and back into the cold.

ST. MICHAEL'S GOLDEN-DOMED MONASTERY
FEBRUARY 18, 2014
EVENING

Katya examines Misha's shoulder. He winces, barely breathing, and Katya exhales for him, as if showing him how. She knows that when she touches the bruised skin he won't know how gentle she is trying to be, and she feels sorry for causing him pain. They were able to do an X-ray, to see that his ribs weren't broken—his heart wasn't in danger of being punctured. He is bruised down the back, along his arm. The medics gave him icepacks, and one was taped against his chest, on his left side, under his heartbeat.

Katya helped give him pain medication to ease the headache she knew he felt. She touches his brow, near the temple, and Misha's eyebrows and lids soften.

Katya watches Misha's face relax, and she knows everything has changed between them because it had.

Katya moves her hands from Misha's brow, and he opens his eyes.

"No, Katya. Don't go."

"Misha, I'm here."

He pretends not to hear her. Something he did when he didn't want to answer a question. Something he did when he didn't want to say whatever he was thinking out loud. Sometimes he met a question with another question, to avoid telling a lie, to avoid facing the truth.

Katya thinks of her parents, who were worried, who she got off the phone with in a hurry, not needing to feign bad reception because the reception was bad—she told them she loved them and then she said she would call again soon.

All Ezra would receive was one text message that said, *Riots in Kyiv—I am safe.*
He did not call. Now, Misha. Here.
"You should go home," he says.
"I will when the war is over."
"The war is just starting," he says. "There will be worse days than this."
"I know."
"Katya," Misha says, "you have to go home."

When she saw Misha arrive in the church battered, her instinct wasn't to stabilize the patient, to assess. Not like the others. She wanted to hold him, to embrace him. She wanted to take him someplace quiet. All that noise outside and inside of her—everything so achingly loud. As she helps Misha, she forgets she is a doctor, and she remembers she is a woman, that she enjoys touch. She is tired of being a doctor, she is tired of being responsible for healing others—her broken husband, her dead son. She is tired of her son being dead.

Her boy, five years old, who liked to kick a ball, who liked to sing, who liked to look at bugs up-close. Her boy, with his little heart no bigger than his fist, his fist no bigger than an unripe tangelo. A little tangelo that squeezed itself to beat, and squeezed itself to beat, beat, beat, but the pump was broken, so the blood went the wrong direction, causing a spill, and his tangelo heart stopped.

Katya wanted to bury her son herself, pick up a shovel, pick up his little limp body, heavier than it had ever been, heavier than when he was born, heavier than when he fainted for the first time, heavier than when she carried him in her belly, bedridden, unable to move. The first time she saw her baby he was bloody and the hottest thing she had ever touched. The last time she saw him, he was frigid, foreign—still and blank and empty as a doll.

As she flashes a light into Misha's blue eyes, the dilation of his pupils, she feels herself begin to cry. She feels herself slipping, trying to hide, and Misha says, "*Katya.*"

"I'm sorry," she says, sobbing. "I'm sorry."

He takes her hand, which feels empty, helpless, pitiful.

Katya watches Misha trace the inside of her palm with his index finger. He studies her palm like a map. She studies his face—he looks older than he is. It wasn't his greying hair, his unshaven jaw. It was in the eyes. The fatigue, the heaviness, there. She wondered if he could feel her pulse—how fast it was beating. He was a bruised man with a bandaged shoulder and a bruised skull, his unpunctured heart beating strong in his unbroken chest.

Misha turns her wrist carefully so her palm faces upward like a blossom. He locks his fingers with hers.

She recognizes it then: her own pulse, the beating of her own ardent heart.

TRADE UNIONS BUILDING
FEBRUARY 18, 2014
EVENING

There's a plume of smoke so large it seems to cover the sky over Maidan. People are rushing away from the fire as Slava pushes toward it, shoving through people, hoping it's the last place that Dascha would have been working, fearing the opposite to be true.

All the bodies flooding against her—it feels like the sea in Odesa where she grew up, and the heat from the fire warms her like the sun. The smoke chokes her. Some men are wearing gas masks and coats, heading into the building, searching for fire extinguishers, for water. She looks up where a group is pointing, and there's a man there, and he's trying to get down.

Jump, they say, holding out their arms. *Jump*. He jumps, and Slava looks away.

It burns. The police use their water cannons not on the fire, but on the people. It's hours later that firefighters arrive. They are trapped, suffocating.

"There's people still in there," others say, pointing upward. Others yell at the Berkut police to use their water cannons on the fire. *Braty!* they say. *Brothers!* And no one answers. The fire roars, unstoppable.

There, she sees her, kneeling beside a man, bloodied and covered in ash, and he's talking about the fire, saying the police started it, the bastards, waving his hands in the direction of the Berkut. Dascha is listening to him and scratching in a notebook balanced on her knee.

Slava runs toward her, bodies pushing her back, back. Dascha embraces her, kisses her ear. Dascha is warm and smells like fire.

The man is bleeding from his skull, and Dascha says to her, "He needs medical attention."

"We'll take him to St. Michael's."

"I will take him," Dascha says. "Meet me at home. Go somewhere safe."

The man looks up at Dascha, then Slava, then spits at the ground.

Лиза, he calls her, pulling away. *Leza.*

Йди до біса, Slava says, pushing him. *Go to Hell,* she tells the old man.

Slava takes Dascha's hand, leaving the bleeding old man, past the bodies and the flames, and she leads her to her apartment on Shovkovychna Street. She doesn't lose her hand, not once, and she wonders, later, if this was the mistake she made. If this had been too bold.

What is the act of love if not bold?

As the world comes apart, nothing to lose—

What is love if not a promise to go on?

Later, when they lift the charred bodies from the wreckage, the skin flakes in the snow. They lay their brothers in the street.

ST. MICHAEL'S GOLDEN-DOMED MONASTERY
FEBRUARY 19, 2014
EARLY MORNING

Misha listens to the Captain, murmuring in his sleep. He stands and goes to him. His own body aches, and his head throbs, but he wants to hear. He wants to hear what he's murmuring.

Misha is startled when he sees that the old man's eyes are already open, light as day, staring at him.

"Mikhail," the old man says. His tongue, lips dry.

"Captain," Misha says. "I thought you were asleep."

"No, no." The old man looks at the ceiling. He moves slow, even his eyes.

"No, no."

Misha realizes how quiet it is. He slides a chair over to the Captain and notices the bodies draped in white sheets. He and the Captain have been put in a room for storing the dead.

"Mikhail," the old man says. Misha sits beside the old man to hear better.

The old man is speaking soft, though his voice graveled.

Misha leans in. "Captain?"

The Captain says, "Mikhail."

"Yes—"

"Misha," the Captain says.

The Captain taps on his chest weakly, "Ivanovich."

"*Мне жаль. Мне жаль,*" the Captain says. Misha covers his own face with his hands. Then he takes the hands of the Captain and he kisses them.

The Captain says, *I'm sorry. I'm sorry.*

OLEG SENTSOV SENTENCED TO 20 YEARS IN LABOR PRISION, INITIATES HUNGER STRIKE

The Ukrainian-Crimean filmmaker has been illegally stripped of his Ukrainian citizenship by the Russian government and was sent to Yakutsk, then to Labytnangi in Siberia in order to serve his 20-year sentence, which has sparked international outrage.

On May 14, 2018, a month before the World Cup was to be held in Russia, Sentsov began a hunger strike in protest of the imprisonment of 64 Ukrainian citizens in Russia.

Today marks the 50th day of the strike and his lawyer, Dmitry Dinze, has reported that Sentsov showed signs of kidney failure two weeks ago during his last visit.

In a letter that Sentsov had smuggled out of prison, he stated:

"If we are supposed to become nails in the coffin of a tyrant, I'd like to become one of those nails. Just know this particular nail will not bend."

AUDIO CASSETTE RECORDING
SIDE ONE CONTINUED

The old piano teacher—the last day he saw me, he said: *Aleksandr, do you know what your name means?*

No, I said, picking up the tools. I pressed down on an ivory key, testing the sound.

Alexander the Great. A conqueror. A killer. The name Alexander *actually means 'Defender of Man.'*

The old teacher knelt to look me in the eyes. He held my shoulders. I had been serving as his eyes, which were gray and fogging, yet he saw so clearly what I didn't.

Aleksandr, he said. *Do you understand what I mean?* I shook my head. I felt inexplicably afraid. For him, for us.

The lion is both a hunter and a protector, Aleksandr. Pride— both a virtue and a vice. He patted my head.

He said, *Take care, son.* And that was all.

[Silence.]

[A tea kettle whistles. A chair creaks, the sound of footsteps away, footsteps near. A chair creaks.]

The Czech hated the Soviets, sweet Anna. Ah, your people—your mother's people—such passionate people. I hadn't expected the crowds, the fires, the protest, the boys being thrown onto the pavement, arrested. Men and women spat in my face. A boy on the tank with me was struck in the jaw with a brick. He cried out, guttural. His jaw heavy, his pain primal as an ape.

That was August 1968. We had encompassed the city. One night, I was patrolling the Charles Bridge on foot and I saw the same woman with short dark hair, mussed by the summer wind. I was alone and she hid in the shadow of a statue, feet touching the edge of the bridge. She was considering whether or not to jump.

Wait— I said, and she startled, balanced herself with her palm on the arched back of the saint. She turned to look at me in the lamplight, her red coat open, revealing a dress. She had been crying a great deal.

He left, she said. *To France. He left me and now you're here.*

Come down from there, I said. *Please.*

He left because of you, she said.

He left because he's a coward, I said. *Another will not make the same mistake.*

She looked down at me. She held out her hand. She was warm, her strength unexpected.

Will you walk me home? She asked me.

I am working, I said.

For how long? she asked.

Until dawn, I said.

She looked at her watch.

Three hours, she said.

She looked away from me, toward the end of the bridge.

You're alone, she said.

For another half-hour.

I have been grieving, she said, coming closer to me. *I'm tired of grief.*

I'm married, I said. *I have a daughter. Back home.* I leaned away from her.

You raped my country, she said. *You're a dog in heat.* She stepped toward me, I stepped away. She was burning.

I'm working, I said, looking at her, direct. *That is all.*

She was silent as she cooled. She circled me, looked my uniform and gun up and down.

What is your name? she asked me.

Ivanovich, I said. She walked toward a large statue, near the end of the bridge. I followed her.

Saint Ivan, she said, gesturing.

He is with two others, she went on. *St. John of Matha and St. Felix of Valois. The three saints who would buy Christian slaves and set them free.*

Beneath the three saints was a jail cell, broken open. Three men in the cave. St. John held chains and money. St. Felix set a man free. St. Ivan sat highest amongst them. Below, a deer with the same cross St. Ivan holds in his hands.

He was a hermit—Ivan, she said. *He was the son of a Croatian king. The patron saint of Slavs.*

How do you know this? I asked.

I like history, she said. *My country's history is dying.*

I looked back at St. Ivan. I felt her eyes on me.

I said to her: *In a pride of lions, when a cub is old enough, he is exiled and cast into the desert alone.*

And how do you know this? she asked. She smiled gently for the first time.

An old teacher, I said. *He taught me many things. And then he was gone.*

We both looked up at Ivan. I did not think of my father.

My commanding officer returned from his break. He saw me standing with the woman and called me over. I told him how I had found her.

Walk her home, he told me. *Stay with her. It's most important we anticipate what is coming.* I stared at him. I tried to hide my trembling. I wanted to protest. I thought of my child, my wife. I was the son of Arkady Ivanovich—hero of the war.

Find me tomorrow afternoon, he said. I walked back to the woman, heart in my throat. And she stood there, waiting.

It has been a long day, I said to her. I took off my hat. I thought of my child. I thought of my wife. The party where I had met her, when she said: *You wear that uniform too well, Sasha Ivanovich.*

I said to the woman on the bridge: *I need some relief. Walk with me.*

She took my arm. Then, she led us away.

SHOVKOVYCHNA STREET
FEBRUARY 19, 2014

When Dascha was a girl, her best friend Inna disappeared.

They were twelve years old. Dascha and Inna played dolls, kissed, held hands. Inna was walking home from school one day and hadn't come home. First, they suspected truancy—a natural response. Then, they suspected kidnapping, the sex trade. Inna's mother walked all over the village, telling children to go home, shining a flashlight when dusk came.

She yelled at them, "This is how young girls disappear! Get inside, get inside."

Inna became a ghost. Dascha saw her sometimes in her dreams.

When Dascha was older, maybe twenty, while she went to the university, she thought she saw Inna crossing the street one night. She couldn't be sure because she had not seen Inna in quite a long time, and she was in a car with new friends—but the girl was tall, thin, and the headlights lit her up like a candlestick, her legs long in her skirt, her eyes wide as a fawn's. Dascha's friend honked the horn as she crossed, not in a hurry, not afraid of being hit. The girl kept her arms in her jacket, not looking up again.

Nights later, Dascha was helping her mother with dinner when she learned that a girl her age had been kidnapped not far from the club Dascha and her friends had gone to that night. She didn't hear it on the news, but from her mother.

"What did she look like?" Dascha asked.

"I don't know. Tall, brunette. My heart dropped when I heard—I thought it could have been you, but you were already asleep in bed."

"Did you hear her name?"

Her mother shook her head. "You will please be careful, Dascha," her mother had said. Dascha felt as if Inna had died twice. She took it as an omen. She carries mace with her, always aware of who might be following. At Maidan, journalists are not safe, and besides the early walks in the morning, she is typically never completely alone. She knows this as a woman, first, and a journalist, second.

She leaves Slava's apartment early, while it is still dark, in order to meet a contact to discuss a cryptic message she received from an editor she occasionally freelanced for, suggesting that she return to Crimea. She barely slept the night before, uneasy at what the message implied. She left a note on the kitchen table as she always has, near the chair where Slava has her coffee. Just in case. The killings, the shootings. It was too dangerous. She will not go to Maidan, but she needs fresh air.

She walks down the steps and pushes open the heavy building door. She crosses the courtyard, but before she gets to Shovkovychna she hears something, and walks faster.

They grab her. Despite her strength, one puts a bag over her head. It's dark, suffocating. She kicks, tries to scream, but she can't break free. She can't. She hears the doors of a vehicle open and she begins to cry.

Get inside, get inside.

No, she screams. *No—*

JOURNALIST DASCHA BANDURA
REPORTED MISSING
FEBRUARY 20, 2014

Ukrainian journalist, Dascha Bandura, has been reported missing and was last seen at 5 a.m. near Shovkovychna Street where she was staying at the home of a friend.

Bandura has been reporting on a number of events at Maidan and published a short film on the Automaidan just weeks before her disappearance.

Any information on Bandura's whereabouts should not be reported to local police.

THE HEAVENLY HUNDRED: LIST OF PROTESTORS KILLED DURING THE REVOLUTION OF DIGNITY AT MAIDAN IN KYIV, UKRAINE 2013–2014

Vasyl Aksenin
Reshat Ametov
Georgiy Arutiunyan
Oleksandr Badera
Serhiy Baidovsky
Oleksandr Baliuk
Ihor Batchinsky
Ivan Bliok
Serhiy Bondarchuk
Serhiy Bondarev
Volodymyr Boykiv
Oleksiy Bratushko
Valeriy Brezdenyuk
Olha Bura
Volodymyr Chaplinsky
Andriy Chernenko
Victor Chernets
Dmytro Chernyavskiy

Viktor Chmilenko
Serhiy Didych
Ihor Dmytriv
Antonina Dvoryanets
Andriy Dyhdalovych
Mykola Dziavulsky
Petro Hadzha
Ustym Holodnyuk
Ivan Horodniuk
Maksym Horoshishin
Eduard Hrynevych
Roman Hurik
Bohdan Ilkiv
Bohdan Kalyniak
Oleksandr Kapinos
Serhiy Kemsky
Viktor Khomyak
Artur Khuntsaar

Zurab Khurtsia

David Kipiani

Volodymyr Kishchuk

Andriy Korchak

Anatoliy Korneyev

Ihor Kostenko

Mykhailo Kostyshyn

Yevhen Kotliar

Vitaliy Kotsyuba

Ivan Kreman

Volodymyr Kulchytskyi

Anatoliy Kurach

Dmytro Maksymov

Maksym Mashkov

Artem Mazur

Pavlo Mazurenko

Volodymyr Melnychuk

Andrii Movchan

Vasyl Moysey

Ivan Nakonechny

Volodymyr Naumov

Yuriy Nechiporuk

Serhiy Nigoyan

Roman Nikulichev

Oleksandr Khrapachenko

Roman Olikh

Valeriy Opanasyuk

Dmytro Pahor

Mykola Pankiv

Yuriy Parashchuk

Yuriy Paskhalin

Volodymyr Pavliuk

Ihor Pehenko

Oleksandr Plekhanov

Leonid Polyansky

Vasyly Prohorskiy

Viktor Prokhorchuk

Andriy Sayenko

Oleksandr Scherbatyuk

Mykola Semisiuk

Roman Senyk

Ihor Serdyuk

Serhiy Shapoval

Oleksandr Shcherbaniuk

Vasyl Sheremet

Liudmyla Sheremeta

Viktor Shvets

Yosyp Shylinh

Maksym Shymko

Taras Slobodian

Vitaliy Smolinsky

Bohdan Solchanyk

Serhiy Synenko

Ivan Tarasiuk

Mykola Tarshchuk

Igor Tkachuk

Roman Tochyn

Volodymyr Topiy

Oleksandr Tsariok

Andriy Tsepun

Oleh Ushnevych

Bohdan Vaida

Roman Varenytsia

Vitaliy Vasyltsov

Yuriy Verbytskyi

Vyacheslav Veremiy

Vyacheslav Vorona

Nazar Voytovych

Yakiv Zaiko
Anatoliy Zhalovaha
Andriy Zhanovachiy
Volodymyr Zherebniy
Anatoliy Zherebnyh
Mikhail Zhiznevsky
Vladyslav Zubenko
Volodymyr Zubok

SUPREME COUNCIL OF UKRAINE, VERKHOVNA RADA, REACTS
SUNG BY KOBZARI

On February 21, 2014, the Heavenly Hundred are recognized by
the Ukrainian Parliament.
We honor their deaths, singing in union a Lemko folk song:
My dear mother, what will happen to me
if I die in a foreign land?

Oh, my dearest
you will be buried by strangers.

The dead rest in caskets and we lift the caskets through the crowd.
We light candles, holding them with cupped hands, protecting
from the wind.
From above, it looks like a mirror of the night sky. A pool
reflecting the stars.

We hold a vigil and the photos of the lost are lined with flowers, notes, rosary, ribbons. We carry our brothers in caskets. We
carry our brothers. We lay our brothers in the street. We lay our
brothers in the earth.

President Yanukovych flees Ukraine to seek asylum in Russia. Our constitution is restored. We begin to pack the tents. We begin to remove the barricades. We lie sleepless in our beds.

Ah, ah—
No, no, my friend. It's not over.
You will see.

PROCESSION OF THE SAGE

Aleksandr Ivanovich watches Katya tend to Misha out of the corner of his red, tired eyes. He sees their hands clasped together tight like a bud. Aleksandr wants to reach out. To fold his hands over theirs as if he were a priest. But he cannot reach.

Katya leaves. It is only Aleksandr and Misha. Misha comes close, takes his hand. Aleksandr Ivanovich closes his eyes.

The Buddhists teach: to avoid suffering, let your thoughts be clouds, passing by—

Aleksandr Ivanovich remembers the augurs of spring.

AUDIO CASSETTE RECORDING
END OF SIDE ONE

I returned to Moscow a criminal in my own mind.

Nedezdha met me at the train station alone—our daughter at home with her *baba*. It was cold and the winter had arrived. Her freckled cheeks reddened from the cold, my Nadia kissed me, and I fell at her feet.

Sasha, she cried. *Are you okay?*

I kissed her gloved hands and she knelt with me in the snow as onlookers passed, watching.

What's happened? she whispered.

I told her about the woman on the bridge, the officer, the order. I told her I was a coward—that I had betrayed her. She wiped the snow from her face and pulled me up.

Come, Sasha, she said, without gentleness. I followed her to the car.

You'll never do that again, she said, turning to me after the doors were slammed closed.

I promise, I said.

No, I mean out there—and she motioned toward the station. *In front of those people—you are a Soviet soldier, Aleksandr Arkadyevich Ivanovich. The greatest army in the world. You will not ever disgrace me like that again.*

I must have looked shocked, stunned stupid. I felt it.

You did what you needed to do, Sasha, Nadia said to me. *With the Czech woman. You followed your commanding officer.*

I started to protest, but she said to me, *It was your work and your duty. To the State. To us. And all of us.*

When I said nothing, Nadia turned on the car. She smiled at me and said: *Wait until you see all that has changed.*

152

FEBRUARY 26, 2014
MORNING

Not long ago, Slava sat in Misha's apartment's open window, smoking. She wore only a t-shirt and underwear and she didn't look at him. She looked outside at Kyiv, where she had rebuilt her life. At the time, she had considered moving to France with FEMEN.

"Will you wait for me, brother? Will you wait for me, my love?" she asked. A sardonic smile. She remembers feeling beautiful in this memory.

But Misha didn't say anything. He watched her from the bed, fell back and away, stared at the ceiling. He didn't say anything, she realizes now, because he knew she would not go.

Now, she begins to pack. Unsure of whether she will ever return to Kyiv, she brings only her favorite clothing. She cleans the kitchen, the bathroom. She dusts and sweeps. She waters the plants above the sink where Dascha rinsed her hair. She folds the stained pillowcase, lays it carefully in her bag. She calls for a ride.

She does not contact Misha until she's in Odesa. She leaves him a message. She calls her father to tell him that she is coming to see him, but he does not answer. She texts Adam to confirm he will meet her there.

She'd called Dascha nearly a hundred times in seven days. She felt unable to eat, unable to stay awake. It felt impossible—the suddenness and vastness of her vacancy. Slava paced around the apartment, curled into herself. She felt like a skeleton. She felt already dead.

She longs to be dead.

When she thinks about death, she calls Dascha.

Dascha says, *Zalyshte meni povidomlennya—*

Leave me a message—

The last time Slava calls, she is in Odesa. Slava whispers into the receiver:

я тебе люблю—

I love you.

Loss, when it occurs, has memory stronger than the mind, stronger than visual recollection patterned in the brain. It's something the flesh knows, the muscles know, like a dancer reciting a step done hundreds of times, like a musician playing a song or a scale after decades without practice. It's something the body knows, something the body is aware of while the mind adapts, responds, reacts.

When she gets off the train in Odesa to meet the American, Slava pulls the collar of her coat up to warm the chill on her neck.

In the cold, near the spray of the sea, Slava thinks of her mother.

PART II

ЧАСТЬ II

ЧЕРНОБИЛ
WORMWOOD

And the name of the star is called Wormwood:
and the third part of the waters became wormwood;
and many men died of the waters,
because they were made bitter.

—Revelation 8:10-11

THE EXCLUSION ZONE

encircles the land around Chernobyl. This is where Reactor 4 burned for ten days, where Vera's father died instantly, where thousands of people were evacuated from their homes in 1986.

The area is approximately 1,000 square miles or 2,600 square kilometers. Five thousand employees still arrive in Chernobyl, working fifteen days in, fifteen days out, to keep the radiation in their bodies leveled. Tourists stay in Soviet-style hotels nearby, getting tours of the power plant from guides.

On one of these tours, a man asks the guide to take the group to the most contaminated spot. He kneels, offers a ring. She covers her mouth. She cries and embraces him. The witnesses clap, whoop, and smile.

Life, they say, *goes on.*

PRIPYAT, UKRAINE
MARCH 20, 2014

The air smells clean, Katya thinks, window cracked, the air doming Chernobyl, rushing in. Misha drives. It's been nearly one month since the protests have ended. It's raining. It is a beautiful evening.

She looks at the passing trees, barren. She looks at Misha, who glances at her. He forces a smile. *He looks afraid*, she thinks. Or at least nervous. She thinks about reaching out to hold his hand, but she is still technically married and it doesn't seem right. So she doesn't touch him. She leaves him to comfort his own thoughts.

Ezra, when Isaac died, wanted to fuck out his misery. He would reach for her in the night and she'd let him. It never relieved her, not in the way it relieved him. The distraction wasn't the act—they rarely had sex after they had a child, and it seemed unnatural to have sex only because Isaac was gone. She resented Ezra when she thought this, when he reached out for her in the evening. She twisted a narrative that said, *he's glad he's dead so now he has you all to himself—so he can fuck again*. Katya would turn away from her husband after he came. And then when she returned home from the hospital, she began sleeping on the couch, *so as not to disturb him*.

She loved her husband, still. Katya knows this, watching the trees pass. The world a storm. The world underwater.

"Are you nervous to see her?" Katya asks Misha, who studies the road.

"Is it silly if I say yes?" he says.

"No," Katya says. "I would be nervous to see my mother, too." She smiles at him. A bad orphan joke.

"What would you do if you found out who your birth mother was?" Misha asks. "Would you go find her?"

"It feels like cheating," Katya replies. "On my mother."

"What about your father?"

"I suppose it would be the same. Though my birth father didn't carry me, didn't birth me. I wonder what it was like, for a mother to give her child away."

"Are you angry with her?"

"Can I tell you something crazy?"

"Yes."

"I am angry with everyone."

Misha reaches for her hand and holds it. Tight.

They pull up to a sentry post and a tall guard examines her and Misha, before speaking in Russian to Misha. The rain pours. Katya reads the warning signs, in Ukrainian and English:

CARE!

Radiatin effected area
Chernobyl zone
Restricted territory
Unothorized entry
BANNED:

Tresspassers incur
administrative penalty and
criminal responsibility
pertinent to the
Laws of Ukraine

Katya notices a tour bus driving toward the gate. *Chernobyl Tours*, it advertises. Misha argues with the guard. She takes from her wallet the *hryvnia* she withdrew from the ATM. The U.S. dollar goes a long way in Ukraine. She touches Misha's arm and he looks at her. He shakes his head and tells her *nyet* in Russian, waving her away, before turning back to the guard. Katya opens the passenger door and approaches the guard, rain falling hard.

"Passport?" the guard says.

She removes it from her coat. He opens the passport under his umbrella. The bills are folded inside. The guard looks behind him, at the guardhouse, and holds the bills between his fingers. He holds up the passport picture and tells Katya to take off her glasses. She raises her hands to take them off, her hair soaked, sticking to her neck. Misha, aggravated, gets out of the car and tells the guard to quit with the game. The guard laughs, pats Misha on the back. He gives Katya back her money, her passport. He apologizes to her and opens the passenger door of the car.

"Rich Americans, always thinking the dollar will solve their problems. Sometimes, yes. Bribe here, bribe there. Helps a man make a living. But more than money, is family," the guard says to her in Russian. "Misha is a brother to me."

He kisses Misha's forehead. The guard waves them through.

"He checks in on my mother," Misha says. "He lost his father, too. His mother is still alive. Lives down the street from mine."

"What were you arguing about? I couldn't hear."

"He was upset I hadn't told him I had a girlfriend. And he scolded me for not calling my mother while I was at Maidan."

"Am I your girlfriend?"

"You know I can't answer that."

They both fall quiet. Misha pulls the car over to the side of the road, parks. He turns to her.

"We can turn around," he says. "Anytime. Now would be best—the further we go on, the more radiation there is, the closer we get to Pripyat."

"I want to go. I want to see where I was born. Where my mother adopted me. The last place my birth mother was, the last place where she saw me."

Misha keeps his eyes on hers. "Going there—it will not bring her to you. It may only disappoint you. You understand?"

"I've lost my family," Katya says to Misha. "I've lost them all." And that is all she can manage.

Misha turns toward her. He leans into her, and touches her face, wet from the rain. He pulls her bangs from her brow, away from her eyes. He whispers, "I don't trust people who have never felt loss."

When he turns on the car, Katya looks at the road ahead, darkening from the setting sun.

MAY DAY, 1986
SUNG BY KOBZARI

We evacuated our homes, holding bundles. Our men collapse like horses. It is not the first time.

On May Day in Kyiv, there is still a parade. Women smile, flowers in their hair—ribbons and posters, raised arms. Everywhere, Lenin.

We watch it on television while rubbing the backs of our children as they vomit paste into a bucket.

Our husbands shoveled the reactive waste, their skin blackened, faces puffed.
The cracked skin, pink flesh peeling like split fruit.
Tastes like metal, our children say while treated for cancers.

Some of the old ones return home, tending familiar soil, eating mushrooms, canning jams.
They live for decades. They flourish.

What's so bad about it? the old ones ask. *Water is just as fresh. Berries just as sweet.*
We, those who have moved away, in anguish, say:

Not even the famine killed us—
Not even the war—

And oh—now we will die alone
in a foreign land.

PRIPYAT, UKRAINE
MARCH 20, 2014

In the dark, he spots the glowing lights inside. The outline of his mother in the window, waiting. He and Katya step outside the car and Misha takes the bags. He can hear music playing, faintly. An old cassette of Olga Pavlova. His mother's favorite. He can hear her singing—how he missed her voice.

She'd shown him how to read music, but it was Vera who had shown him how to play—her thin fingers on the neck of a guitar. *Like this*, she'd say, adjusting his fingertips on the strings. Misha liked to pretend to make mistakes so she would correct him.

Now, before they walk to the door, Katya touches the small of his back, near the belt. Her hand feels as if it's always meant to be there, on him, guiding and following at once.

His mother opens the door and cries, *Mikhail, my son, my son*, and she wraps her large arms around him, enveloping him like a blanket. She sees Katya and her eyes widen in joy, in hope, in silent prayer. She opens the door wide and they are welcomed into the cottage by the warm and the dry.

His mother fusses over them, warming the borscht, the bread. She isn't wearing her scarf, and her hair is thinning. Her fingers and wrists are thicker now, her arms and face browned from working in her garden.

"You will see in the morning," his mother says, standing in the kitchen, Misha and Katya at the small table. "The berries, the way they thrive here. The bushes are full, so full they are heavy. We will pick them, together. You would like that? We can make fresh jam."

Misha looks at Katya, who smiles. "I would love to see your garden," Katya says.

"It is her pride and joy," Misha says, eyes flickering, mischievous. "The garden is her favorite child. It doesn't talk back."

His mother turns from the stove, red from the steam. She waves the spoon at him. "Ah, the garden talks. She tells me the sun is warm, the water is fresh, the soil is soft. She tells me, she shows me, 'Look at the earth! Look at how she lives! They said it was dead, this land. They said it was poison!' You will see," she says to Katya, "how beautiful the garden is."

Around them are old black-and-white photographs—his grandmother's things. Photos of Misha's mother as a child, round-faced and joyful. He sees the marriage photos of his mother and father, grandmother and grandfather, great-grandmother and great-grandfather. Photos of great-grandfather in the war. The embroidered towels draped behind the photographs. The stitching of berries blood red and black, the flowers blue and gold, generations old and yellowed, the *rushnyk* made by a girl long ago. Wooden carvings his grandfather and great-grandfather made, whittling on the porch, to keep their hands out of trouble. The crystal vase—a wedding gift when his mother was married—is filled with wilting flowers, the water slicked with algae. Misha makes a note to replenish them, to clean the vase.

"I've made your old room, Misha," his mother says, after they have eaten, cleared the table. "I did not know there would be a guest—"

"Let Katya take my bed, Mama. I'll sleep here, on the couch."

His mother wipes her brow, distressed by the lack of communication, by the surprise guest Misha knows has both pleased and confused her. She looks at her son, and he can feel her heart.

"Let me get the blankets, the pillows—" she goes to the armoire, framed by bookshelves, filled with books, and Misha takes what she hands him. Olga Pavlova clicks. The end of side one. It is 11:35 p.m. His mother rubs her eyes, and she looks like a little girl. How much he loves her. How old she is becoming.

"Go to sleep, Mama," he says. "I'll show Katya her room. We'll turn in, soon."

She nods, quieter, slower now that she's tired. He stands up, and it's his turn to eclipse her, walking to her room, and she pats his back, wipes her eyes.

She turns to Katya and says, "This is my son, and I love him more than anything."

Katya nods at her, understanding.

The two of them, alone. They've made tea. Misha goes through the cassettes on a bookshelf, searching for something to replace Olga Pavlova. Katya looks over his shoulder, reading the titles. There are hundreds, it seems.

"It's been so long since I've seen a cassette tape," she says. "Longer since I've listened to one."

Misha can feel her warmth without touching. He can sense her without feeling her. And he likes her, there. "So many of these came after the USSR. We didn't have access to much American music, but since then, my mother became a fanatic." He takes out a tape—Celine Dion. There's Michael Jackson. The Beatles. Tchaikovsky. Queen. Journey.

"She listens to all of these?" Katya asks.

"When the wall came down, we listened to everything," Misha says. "I started bringing them to her, anything I could find. She doesn't understand much English, so she listens for the melody and the voices." He takes out Shania Twain. "This is her favorite," he says. He puts it into the player, snaps it closed.

They listen, eyes locked. When the track plays, Misha grins.

Man! I feel like a woman!

Katya erupts into laughter, throwing back her head. He notices one filling on a top molar. He finds himself joyful at what he's never noticed before, having never seen her this way. A small mole under the jaw, near the base of her neck. He has an urge to know all of her. The cartography of her, what's hidden.

Katya drinks her tea, still fighting her laughter, and finds a tape.

"Bruce Hornsby and the Range?" She picks it off the shelf. Misha puts the tape in.

"This came out the year we moved to L'viv," Katya said. "Dad had this one, and others, smuggled in. I was adopted, then we moved. It was the beginning of the end, anyway. In '91, he blasted it as loud as the walls could take it, Mom said. Then we moved to the United States."

Misha flips over the case, reading. "Nineteen eighty-six."

Katya nodded. "Big year, this part of the world."

"When did you move? The month?"

"We moved to Kyiv two weeks earlier, mid-April. I remember because it was just after my birthday."

A silence. Misha looks at the cassette player. Bruce Hornsby and the Range plays on.

"You were here," she asks him, "that day. You left, right after? That night?"

"A little later," he tells her. "My father still needed to work."

Misha's father, an engineer, had been called to examine the damage of the fire. They put him inside a helicopter, hovering over Reactor 4. They dared not fly directly above. He said he felt like a moth in a plume.

His father came home that night and the plume lingered and merged into rain clouds. Acid rain burned the forests, the beasts covered in scabs, in tar. The families in Pripyat were evacuated from their homes. Most of Misha's friends from school went to Belarus and Misha never saw them again.

His family went to the funerals and memorials of the men who had died. Misha squeezed his father's hand, glad his father was still alive. It was a year later while living in Kyiv that his father passed away.

"Vera's father was killed instantly, inside the reactor. I felt guilty that my father had survived."

But it was the plume that killed his father—not the explosion. It was the plume that seeped into his father's body, into his cells, it took ahold at the base of his throat.

"The doctor gave my father a picture of the moth inside him—the shape of the mass. That's what it looked like. A moth."

Misha's father, a man of science, brought it home to show his wife and son. Misha's mother cried, slammed the bedroom door, unable to listen.

"I stayed with him," he says. "I looked at the black-and-white image with my father."

Misha's father sat at the dinner table and drew his son a simple map of Chernobyl. He showed where the fire started and how far the smoke had traveled. He explained how things went wrong and how they should have functioned, as he understood. Misha's father took off his glasses, placed them near his glass of vodka and rubbed his eyes.

You need to know this, Mikhail, his father said. *You must know that all actions have consequences. Everything in life is an experiment. There is always something to be understood that wasn't understood before. There is always cause and effect. There is always something to be learned.*

After his father died, Misha and his mother moved in with Vera's family. They moved to Dnipropetrovsk. It was difficult for Misha's mother. She promised one day she would return home.

"That first year in Dnipropetrovsk, Vera and I went to the river a lot. That's where we truly became close. It was the beginning of us, there."

Misha would teach Vera about the river, the Dnieper. He knew many things about it because of his father, who had taught Misha about the ecosystem: the plants, bugs, algae. Their dog, Dracula, would sniff the grass, and Misha would peer into the water, fish nibbling on the rocks.

His father had told him about microorganisms, the composition of air, and the cells that made up Dracula's tongue. After his father was gone, Misha taught Vera about these things, lying on the beach in the sun.

Misha loved his father and missed him. But that first year, when he was nearly twelve years old, Vera kissed him in her swimsuit while the wind lifted the gulls.

"I would tell myself, 'this wouldn't have been possible, would it, had Dad lived?' It was my way of thinking it was a blessing, somehow. A way of accepting his death. That maybe it was God's design. But what kind of God is that? Tit-for-tat. Your father or your wife?"

His mother always told him, *God has a plan.* So Misha made his own plans. He went to college, became an engineer. Vera went to a conservatory to play the violin.

A long time ago. A lifetime, it seemed. A dream.

And now he was back in his grandmother's home, now his mother's home, and his wife has been years dead. Here, now, he tells Katya all this, and she listens to him, near him, tilting her head quietly, a presence of peace, while her long hair falls on her neck, her shoulders, her chest, dark and wild. He is struck by her, the fact of this woman being with him, who had lived so near him thirty years ago when the reactor blew. Near him, near Vera.

Katya steps closer to him, slides her finger into a beltloop near his hip, and pulls.

Meanwhile, Bruce Hornsby sings, *That's just the way it is.*

HOW TO MAKE LOVE TO
A MAN NOT YOUR HUSBAND

You will lead him because he will not lead you. Even though the ring is gone, your husband is always in the room, until you mentally push him out.

When you kiss this man, it will feel new and old at once—it will taste like a familiarity you've missed, a familiarity that frightens you, and the response, the way he responds to you, tongue and teeth, turns you on.

You'll fumble, and the first time you will both be mostly dressed, his jeans unbuttoned, your jeans unzipped taut around your thighs, but his cold hands will slide up your back, over your breasts, and your belly will kiss his. You'll have to guide him, but he finds your fingertips, and while he's inside you, he's also listening by feeling, by following—and you tell him, his rough jaw buried in your neck, that you want him to make you come, and he'll say, *show me*—

When you grow near, he's watching you and you don't feel shy, you don't feel afraid. You want him to see you, you want him to see all the parts of you, every part of you, everything broken and torn and stretched and sewn. You want him to see you come, you want him to see you widen, expand—you want him to see what he's done to you, what he's capable of doing, of making you *feel good*—

And it feels good—it feels good to have him inside of you, it feels good to have his teeth pinch your breast, his tongue tracing, his fingertips slicked with you, with him, as he sends you— he sends you—and it feels good, being touched, being loved this way, being touched this way, being this way, with this man, with this man who could love you this way, who has given you this gift, this gift of sending you, his body with your body, his sex with your sex, his hands locked with your hands as he sends you, as you send him...

The quiet comes, and you look at one another, tears in your eyes, in his eyes. And you say nothing, and he says nothing, because neither of you know, in his radioactive bedroom, on his radioactive sheets, with his radioactive semen, and your now radioactive womb, if you will ever make love like this again.

Instead, you hum him a song they would sing in the fires of Maidan. He lies on top of you as you comb his hair with your fingers, and you hum, and he closes his eyes, his temple on your clavicle, your whole heart beating—

The pine and fir are burning,
A boy has loved me from afar.

AUDIO CASSETTE RECORDING
SIDE TWO

Spring. Every bud a burst. An eruption. Think of when a child is born: that is how spring enters the world. The cataclysmic joy of Demeter as Persephone returns to earth.

Stravinsky knew it. In *The Rite of Spring*, The Procession of the Sage, the symphony strikes like a hammer, again and again. It pounds—

That is how my first daughter entered the world: violent, red, screaming.

And then the Sage falls to his knees and kisses the ground, and the whole tribe turns upward to look to the gods.

Nadia loved her so tenderly, the way she carried her in her belly and later in her arms, the way she wrapped her in her cradle. Nadia was made to be a mother—it was her sacred joy, her holy purpose. To mother us all.

When we married, she wanted a child right away. I hadn't yet gone to Prague, and she was hungry for life. She was still dancing in the ballet with Anna, and she would soon go to Cuba.

"I want to have your child," she said to me, nights before she left. I wondered so many times before why it mattered to people to have children.

Anna—how she loved Nadia. When they arrived in Havana, Nadia called me and she said, *Sasha, Anna is here. Yes, yes—she is well! Oh, Sasha—she is holding my hand now because I am shaking. I was so ill on the plane, but I am well, now. I have been to the doctor. Yes, everything is well! Oh, Sasha—*

God made us in His image—my old piano teacher had said.

And so, on the phone, Nadia told me we had made a child, and when she was born, we named her Zoya.

When Nadia returned from Cuba, everything was done to keep my dear Nadia healthy. Our mothers fed her, made her strong and walked her. She was radiant, proud.

I remember the night I met her—looking much the same way—in the home of the Bolshoi director, when she wore her blond hair back, her green eyes large and smiling. She laughed in the midst of a group and I caught her eye. She saw me in my army uniform, arm in arm with Anna, and she came over to us.

Who is this? Nadia asked Anna, touching her arm.

This is my brother, Aleksandr. Sasha, this is Nedezdha.

She held out her hand to me, and I took it.

Nadia, she said.

Anna pinched my side, and she left us alone, together. We stayed that way as long as God allowed.

When I returned to Moscow, Zoya was nearly two years old. I kissed her head of curls, pale like her mother's. She clung to Nadia, who held her on her lap. Nadia looked small compared to the growing girl, but she was still a dancer in her musculature. The arms that held our daughter had oftentimes held me, held others. The feet that held her up were callused and rough. Her soles were sandstone, her ankles fine as karst. And our daughter, Zoya, was volcanic—joyful, tearful, laughing, crying.

For five years, while I secretly trained in the KGB, while I performed in the symphony, our daughter grew. She had started dancing lessons with other children and Nadia and Anna would play with her: prima ballerina, where Zoya was the soloist—a Russian princess.

I want to be the Sugar Plum Fairy, she said to Nadia as she watched her Aunt Anna perform the role. Nadia kissed her little hands, saying she would taste so divinely sweet.

And Papa will be the prince, Zoya whispered. The curtain closed. She squeezed my hand in the dark.

And so, we were very happy.
Until.
Always, until.

ODESA, UKRAINE
FEBRUARY 27, 2014

Adam is waiting for her at the airport when she lands.

"Hello," he says, his smile sympathetic. Americans are always smiling for no reason. Still, Slava thinks he is more sensitive than she remembered. He takes her bag, freeing her of the weight.

"Are you hungry?" he asks. "You must be. Dinner? Then hotel?"

Slava nods and smiles back at him. She takes his hand. Slava knows that sometimes, a man wants you to touch him without asking. Sometimes, a woman does, too. Slava wants to be touched.

She is thankful for Adam and Misha.

When she called Misha to tell him she had gone back to Odesa, maybe America, he tells her to travel safely. He says, *I love you, Slava,* for the first time, then, *Stay safe.*

When she called Adam, she told him everything. Of Dascha, their relationship, her plans to leave Kyiv. He had already known about the disappearance. He tried to meet her in Kyiv, but she needed to go, now. Adam says to her, *I'm sorry, Slava.* Then, *How can I help?*

There are protests in Odesa, too. Anti-Maidan protesters incite further aggression. Yanukovych is gone, disappeared to Russia, and pro-Russians come to the streets.

At dinner, Slava drinks water from a glass. Adam sits across from her. Adam has the grilled squid with vegetables. Slava has mussels in white wine.

"My sister is arriving tomorrow," Adam says in Russian. He always speaks to her in Russian. Slava feels as if for the first time she's noticing just how good his Russian is. "Alexis always wanted to come back to Ukraine," Adam says. "We haven't been since we were children."

"Is your family Russian?"

"I haven't told you my mother is Russian? I'm surprised I didn't mention it. Alexis is arriving in Kyiv today to handle a death in the family. An estranged uncle. We are all reeling from it. I wish we could have all met there and traveled here together."

"I had to leave," Slava says. "I couldn't stay. Thank you, Adam."

"It's nothing," he says. "I'm only sorry to be here so briefly. It's important I meet her, though. We'll be back to get you. Alexis and I."

Slava nods, distracted.

"Where was your mother from?" she asks.

"Moscow," he says.

"Has your sister been," she asks, "to Moscow?"

"Yes, my sister and I went once. But not with my mother. She refuses to go back."

"Why?"

"Her family—my grandparents and uncle—are dead. It is a fascinating history. I think she is the reason why I have loved reporting and telling others' stories."

"That sounds like a sad story," Slava says. She feels it swell up inside her. Sadness.

"Most Russian stories are," Adam says, gently. "Alexis and I tried to find their graves. They don't exist."

"How do you know they are dead?"

"My mother has suspected for a while," he said, "but I think we're still unraveling the truth. That seems like the same situation for everyone, here."

"Dascha would have said it's the only path worth pursuing."

Adam lifted his wine glass. "To Dascha," he says.

Later, she lies in bed next to him. Fully clothed, she just wants to feel near someone. Warm, safe. He tucks her hair behind her ear, holds her. Allows her to cry, helps her to laugh.

"I have to meet my father," she says. "To say goodbye."

"Okay," Adam says. "And then we will be off."

She looks at him and smiles but she wonders if she will do it. She wonders if she will make it that far. If she will make it as far as the tarmac. As far as the gate.

Her mother, when she left, never looked behind her. She never cracked the door, never kissed her one last time. She thinks about her mother leaving Ukraine and she wonders if she was ever afraid. Or if she was too stupid to care.

MALAYSIA AIRLINES FLIGHT MH17 CRASHES IN EAST UKRAINE

FROM THE GUARDIAN

JULY 17, 2014

A Malaysia Airlines passenger jet carrying 295 people from Amsterdam to Kuala Lumpur has crashed in an area of eastern Ukraine where separatist rebels have been engaging Ukrainian military forces in recent weeks. Ukraine's president, Petro Poroshenko, said the jet may have been shot down.

"We do not exclude that the plane was shot down and confirm that the Ukraine armed forces did not fire at any targets in the sky," Poroshenko said in a statement.

The field next to the tiny rural hamlet where MH17 plunged to the ground was a scene of charred earth and twisted metal. Locals were distressed to find body parts scattered around the scene. The body of what appeared to be a young woman lay about 500 metres from the centre of the crash, while a dismembered foot could be seen on the one road leading through the village.

A strong smell of aviation fuel hung in the air as pro-Russian separatist fighters attempted to secure the area. Ten fire engines remained on the scene after rushing there to extinguish the many blazes caused by the crash.

One local resident, Alexander, said he was working in the field a few hundred metres from its final resting place when he looked up. He feared the aircraft was going to crash on him.

PRIPYAT, UKRAINE
MARCH 31, 2014

Katya is in the garden with Misha's mother, churning berries to make jam. Spring has arrived and the woods have greened. His mother has brought back mushrooms from the woods in a basket. The sun beats warm and Katya wipes her brow with the back of her hand. The juice on her lips from the berries is sweet.

Sometimes, she forgets where she is.

She saw a stag in the woods the other day and she froze. He watched her, black eyes large, lashes long, and she did not move. The rain fell, turning a bit to snow, the edges of him obscured in mist. It was beautiful. She felt as if she were encased in glass, protected.

In the woods while tending to the garden, tucked away, Katya can't imagine it—the ash cloud, the poisoned birds falling from the sky. Misha's mother doesn't tell her about it: the open sores, the pus, the blood, the vomit. She instead tells her about her husband, Misha's father.

"He loved his work," she said. "He would have stayed, to study it, to understand the mistake, had it not been for us."

Misha had gone on a walk. It was something he did daily, now.

"He walks where his father used to," Misha's mother said, the pestle churning in her hands, red and bloodied from the berry pulp.

While he was out walking, she helped his mother with the cooking, the chores and laundry. She felt like a woman from an ancient time. The brilliant sun on her, the smell of the earth, the stickiness of the jam, the old woman singing—she felt free, natural, at peace.

And then Misha would appear through a thicket of trees from the woods and he'd smile and wave. It felt as if she had always been there. As if she had found Eden. An eternal spring.

She had gotten to know him, the cadence of his voice and the timbre. Katya would listen to his voice through his chest, through his lungs, through his heart. She buried herself into him, into the sound of him.

Misha's mother spots Misha walking up to the house in conversation with another man. She nudges Katya, who looks up. It's the guard from the checkpoint. The man who looks after Misha's mother—Petyr.

Misha's mother hums a little song. She says to Katya, "The men are talking about war."

"How do you know?"

"Russia has invaded Crimea, and now Putin will want more."

"Yes. But perhaps Misha won't go," Katya says, unsure.

Misha's mother takes her hand, both of their fingers sticky and red. She feels as if she has melded to the old woman. As if through her touch, she might inherit all that the woman has ever known.

"We come from *Kozak* blood, my dear. Misha's ancestors were all *Kozak*, both sides. He's been waiting for war his whole life without knowing."

Katya catches Misha's eye as he listens to his friend. He smiles at her. She waves.

His mother says, almost as if it were a song: "It won't be long now. Our children are always going off to war."

ODESA, UKRAINE
RESORT
FEBRUARY 28, 2014

"Would you let me write about you? A story? Well, an essay. About meeting you, coming here—the protests, everything," Adam asks her at breakfast. Slava does not feel hungry. She longs for the sea. She longs for the warm sun, the wind. It is still too cold in Ukraine.

"I'm not sure," she says.

"You are a fascinating woman, Slava," Adam says, watching her through his thick frames—glasses Slava has never seen until today. "You've survived so much. FEMEN left, but why did you stay? What has kept you here?"

"I don't know," Slava says. "I thought I was a patriot."

"And you're ready to leave now? When your country is on the brink of civil war?"

"My country is always at war."

"Are you still a patriot?"

Slava drops her fork and looks at him. "Are you interviewing me right now? Is this how you get what you want? You show up someplace and demand it?"

"No," he says. "I'm sorry."

Adam says to her, "Slava, I know you don't need me to get out of here. There would be other ways, or other men. Of course, I want to help. Terrible things have likely happened to Dascha that could have also happened to you. But why leave now? Of all the times you could have gone? What do you want that was different than before?"

Slava thinks of Dascha in her apartment only nights before she disappeared. She thinks of her sleeping and how peaceful she seemed, how light the breath. She thinks of the snow falling and her bare-breasted at the window, peering out and smoking a cigarette.

What do you want, Slava? Dascha had asked her.

Do you want a lover? Or do you want to be in love?

Slava watched her from the bed and smiled.

I want everything, she said. *I want the whole world.* She never said, *I love you,* when Dascha was there to hear it. How could she? She was a coward.

Dascha said, *Are you afraid to be with a woman?*

Slava said, *I'm here with you.*

But out there—plain as day.

I've already gone to jail once, Slava said.

Everything is changing, Slava. At Maidan. Other things could change as well. I can feel it changing.

And now, that confidence—all that honesty? That proverbial baptism? Where is it?

Dascha is dead.

"Slava," Adam says to her again, gently, breakfast getting cold. "What do you want? When you leave here? What do you want your life to look like?"

Her throat tightens and the smell of the sea comes light with the breeze. Looking at the port, she sees the boats docked. Boats docked with bodies filling the hull. Little coffins, floating on the salty sea. Girls who disappear. Girls who return. Girls who betray girls and lead girls up the gangway. Girls taken from their mothers. Girls taken from their fathers. Mothers who sell their daughters. Fathers who never find them.

"Yes," she says to him. "You can write about me. But you need to tell it all."

DONETSK
AUTUMN 2002

In Eastern Ukraine, where brother Russia peeks over often to watch the miners and the engineers and the geologists carve into the earth with their machines to sift out the ore, Misha Tkachenko feels most natural. He worked for the Ukrainian union to ensure the mines were regulated according to the government and international standards. He felt useful, and indeed, he was.

One afternoon he was approached at his desk by his manager, Oleg, who asked him to have a cigarette outside. He followed Oleg, past the front door, down the street, and wondered how far they would walk before Oleg would stop.

"You're a fine worker, Mikhail," Oleg said, hands in his pockets. "I want to treat you to a drink—this is a day for celebration."

They entered the bar and as Misha's eyes adjusted to the dark, Oleg found them a table. He offered Misha a cigarette and ordered two vodkas. Oleg was a large man, made wholly of muscle and bone, his forehead and nose shone. He had thick dark hair that was balding in the back—monstrous teeth encased in a massive mouth.

"Do you enjoy your work, Mikhail?"

Misha inhaled before answering, "Of course."

"You're a very skilled engineer, Mikhail. Careful. Sure. Patient. Do you have many friends in Donetsk?"

"Not many," Misha said.

He returned to his tiny apartment every night, alone, and would call Vera, who was still at the conservatory. He'd return his mother's calls. He kept mostly to himself.

"Your girlfriend back home—you want a family?" Oleg asked, his big mouth smearing to a grin.

Misha nodded. He sent money home each week, his meals small, saving as much as he could for the women he had protected since he was a boy.

"Tell me, Mikhail," Oleg said. "How would you feel about making more money?"

Misha felt himself sweating. His cigarette burned in the ashtray.

"I'm content where I am," Misha said.

Oleg nodded. He paid the bill and rose from his chair. An enormous man, as if he himself were made of iron.

"You let me know, Mikhail," Oleg said, putting on his coat. "The offer stands as long as you do."

RUSSIAN SOLDIERS WITHOUT INSIGNIA INVADE CRIMEA ON FEBRUARY 27, 2014

SUNG BY KOBZARI

So, Russia takes Crimea.

There's a referendum, a Declaration
of Independence for the Republic of Crimea.
The UN condemns it, but Putin flips the bird and builds a bridge.

In the spring of 2014, the Donetsk People's Republic and the
Luhansk People's Republic are formed.
Overnight, Kyiv had fallen asleep in peace and woken up at war.

But—
Ah, my friend, it's not as simple as taking sides.

Think of Berlin:
In one night in August 1961, a wall was built, separating brother
from brother.

Mother from son,
Father from daughter.

And so it is in Ukraine: overnight, our neighbor is our enemy.

But, there is no wall here:
There are only terminals—

Donetsk Airport.
Kerch.
No Man's Land.

When we shoot, we kill a neighbor.
When we shoot, we kill ourselves.

In Ukraine, the umbilical cord becomes the noose.

AUDIO CASSETTE RECORDING
SIDE TWO CONTINUED

The pagans in *The Rite of Spring* sacrifice a woman, the Chosen One, so they might survive as a tribe. I wonder about this often—the individual loss for the collective gain.

I slept with a woman in Prague and my wife did not reject me. She called it my duty. A sacrifice for the State. And still we were able to be happy, to build a life. I had forgotten about my time in Prague and our love became hardier. I loved Nadia and I feared her. I feared her rejection, I feared her disapproval. I ached for her love, and she gave it to me, her forgiveness, her mercy. And so we made love, to try for another child, but the child never came.

Not in time. Not in time to save us.

[A pause.]

Zoya came home from school one day flushed, feverish, with a cough. Nadia undressed her, cooled her with a towel, wrapped her in blankets as Zoya's little body shook. I went to the pharmacy for medicine, but the child cried, in pain, for two days, and on the third, she was quiet except for a hummingbird in her chest, her ribs concave, convex, taut on the bones.

Nadia woke me that night—Zoya's lips had turned blue. She seemed to be drowning before our eyes. We rushed her to the hospital. They tried to feed her air through a tube and antibiotics through her veins.

She has a deadly case of pneumonia, the doctor said.

I held onto Nadia, her head on my shoulder. We slept at the hospital, sitting up.

When we awoke, Zoya had gone, quiet as snow.

[Silence.]

[A chair creaks. The sound of rain.]

We buried our daughter before the first frost came. Nadezdha fell to her knees over her grave, the earth soft and wet and cold, and her mother tried to pull her away, but Nadia pushed her back. Anna held onto my arm, but I couldn't feel a thing in the world. I couldn't feel the cold. I couldn't feel the ache. I watched my wife bury her face in the fresh earth, muddying her cheeks and hair. I watched as if she were an animal fatally shot. I watched my wife clawing at the dirt, kicking it up between her legs, and my sister said to me, shaking me:

Sasha, she needs you, she needs you—

Sasha, my sister said, but I couldn't hear her anymore. I stopped hearing anything but the sound of pounding in the dirt.

I turned away from Nadia and the sound and lifted my face upward. I closed my eyes. I stuck my tongue out. The taste of cold, the dry taste of wind, of a wrung-out tongue. I gagged and vomited in the mud. I vomited on my Soviet boots, and when I turned to look back at Nadia, tears in my eyes, Anna had pulled her off the grave and had fallen to the ground with Nadia in her arms.

Anna, her eyes wild and helpless.

She won't leave her, Anna told me. *Sasha, she won't leave.*

I knelt beside Nadia, touched her chin in my hand. Her hair tangled, her face powdered with dust.

My love, I said. *We must go home.*

She shook her head and cried. I took her hands and I closed my eyes. I touched my forehead to hers. I felt her third eye to mine. Anna sat between us, like a minister, like we were being married again, under a temple of trees.

I prayed:

The Lord is my shepherd. I shall not want—

I shall not want—

I shall not want—

And Nadia, her arms around my neck, allowed me to lift her from the earth.

[Indistinct.]

Four years after I left, I returned to Prague.

ON NUCLEAR POWER

As a young engineer, Misha learned about the atom. The most fundamental unit of matter.
Matter. *What matters in this life?*

Misha once had a father. He once had a wife. He once dreamed of a child.
The atom has a nucleus. A core.
A family has a hearth. A center.
The positive charge of an atom—

An atom, from the Greek, meaning *impossible to cut.*

But Misha knows:
Everything can be cut. Even the atom.

With Katya, Misha feels an undeniable chemistry.

ODESA, UKRAINE
SLAVA'S CHILDHOOD HOME
FEBRUARY 28, 2014

Adam paid for a cab. He sat beside her in the car, outside her father's home.

Overnight, Crimea had been invaded. The war had begun, he would be interviewing migrants, displaced from their homes. This will be the last story for a few weeks, while he helps Slava get settled.

Slava wrote down her address and tore it from a notebook.

"For you and your sister," she said. "You can pick me up here, if you'd like."

The American looks at the dilapidated home that is her father's and the dilapidated others that are next to it.

"Would you like me to walk you up?" he asked.

"No," she said. "I should go alone."

Slava's father does not answer the door when she arrives, though she sees the curtains move. She knocks again. She waits for the cab to turn down the road, far along the path, the mist rolling in from the sea. She turns toward the house, and braces.

"Tato," Slava says, knocking with her knuckles, and then her fist.

"*Tato!*" she yells. And the door opens, her father in the dark, wearing a stained white shirt. He is round, his hair gone, his beard white. He smells like booze. He smells like sweat. She tries not to seem worried for him. She stays angry.

An orange cat runs out of the house. He jingles as he trots away. She has never seen it before. Her father turns his back and Slava picks up her bag.

Inside, the house is unchanged since she was a girl. There are many bottles, which is the same as it's been since her mother left, but otherwise it is remarkably neat. Still the black-and-white and sepia pictures framed in silver, resting over the doily. Still the medals from the war. Still the old blanket knit by her grandmother, and the rosary, and the china. Slava expects for a moment her mother to come in from the garden, hair mussed and windblown.

She turns on a lamp and the sofa is still warm from where he had been sleeping. In the light, her father is jaundiced. In the light, her father has bruises on his arms. He pours them each a drink. He hands her the glass.

"I thought it was her," he says. "You look like her. Except for your hair."

He waves his hand. Slava feared her father's hands. His hands that bruised her arms, that dragged her into the wooden edges of furniture. The hands that pulled her hair. The hands that, the last time she saw him, tried to choke her.

"I thought she had been frozen in time," he says. He drinks. "I thought it was a dream. And it took me a moment to gather myself. If it is her, I thought, what would I say? And I opened the door and it was you."

Slava drinks. "A disappointment."

"No," he said. "I'm relieved."

He pours again, and Slava says to him, "I came here to tell you I'm going to the United States."

He nods as he pours. He does not look at her. She feels her stomach tighten. She feels herself about to run.

She goes on, "I wanted you to know."

His breath is shallow, his face reddens, and he bangs his fists on the table, unsettling the glasses, which fall. Slava jumps up. The booze spills and neither corrects it. Slava doesn't move. The tremor shakes the room.

"She left you. A real mother would have taken you. A real mother would have never allowed you to feel afraid."

Slava can't move. She feels her heart in her ears. She feels like a child. She feels like a ghost. Her hand shakes. His hands shake.

"I'm not going to do this," Slava says. "I'm not going to do this. I am going to leave."

Her father throws the glass at the wall and Slava runs out the door. He is after her, and she feels again like a little girl. She finds the rake and she faces him and she strikes him with the tines.

She strikes him and her father cries, falling onto the grass while the neighbors watch. She looks at them all behind the curtains, inside their homes, and she screams at them.

"Can you see me?" she says. *"Can you see what kind of fucking person I am?"*

Her father moans and stirs. His nose is bloodied and his face is scratched.

The father begets the daughter—the lion begets the lion. Slava helps her father rise and leads him inside.

AUDIO CASSETTE RECORDING
SIDE TWO CONTINUED

When I arrived in Prague the first time, I knew these things:
I loved my wife.
I loved my daughter.
Nothing terrified me more than losing my family.
When I returned:
I had lost my daughter.
I was losing my wife.
My family was cleft. I became a husk. I feared nothing.

When I received my next assignment, the KGB nearly had themselves the making of a perfect agent. If not for Prague.

It was 1975. They needed me to return to the city—a Czechoslovakian underground movement was resurfacing. It was the intelligentsia gathering: the artists, poets, writers. I was to perform in Prague with a regional symphony. I would enter the circle as one of their own, seating myself at their pianos while they smoked and drank in darkened dens lit by dilapidated lamps, the light a little askew, and as a means of showing off I would begrudge the owner for neglecting the beautiful mahogany, or cedar, or rosewood instrument, claiming it was so slightly sharp that I would insist on returning early the next morning.

And while they nursed their hangovers, I would remove the paneling for their barely played pianos and attach one recording device inside the instrument, and one unnoticeable wire under the keyboard for the KGB.

Some homes were more difficult than others. Some didn't have pianos, of course. One had to have an *in*—an entrance point, a door. The urgency to place a device.

The last time I saw Nadia—whole and beautiful—she was in the kitchen with the laundry. The windows had opened, and the sun was coming through, her shoulders hot to the touch. She folded towels, or sheets, I can't remember. I just recall her hands, the wedding band in the light, nails thin from the steam. They smoothed the white fabric, and smoothed it, and smoothed it. We both watched her hands. I waited for her to look at me, but she didn't.

It's time, I said. She smoothed again the fabric with her hands.

We tried, briefly, for another child. We were still young. But it became difficult—the failure. And we hadn't fully healed. How can you ask a mother to open her womb again, after she lost a child to the sickness of the world?

That was the anguish of it. Our daughter's illness didn't just take her from us—it broke us all.

Nadia said, one night, a few weeks before I left for Prague: *If we have another child, there's nothing we can do to protect them. Not in this world. There is nothing that can be done.*

No, I said, staring into the pitch of the ceiling.

I would rather die, she said, *than lose another child.*

I reached for her in the dark. We made love.

And so, in the kitchen one morning, the laundry pinned up like ghosts, I said to her again, *It's time for me to leave, Nadia.*

She looked up from her smoothing and said: *It's happened again. A child.*

There was nothing joyful in her voice when she told me. She looked afraid—as if she might cry. I dropped to my knees and she let me lift her shirt to touch her belly with my palm, to kiss her where she would grow. Her skin was warm and wet from the heat.

I'll be home as soon as I can, I said. I took her shoulders and her sad green eyes were filled with tears.

Have you told your mother? I asked.

She shook her head. *I don't want anyone to know*, she said. *Their faces when I tell them—will they be happy or sad? They will never be completely joyful—how could this happen?*

She was trembling and I brought her a chair to sit. I touched her knee. My Nadia. My poor young love.

We don't need to tell them, I said. *Not until you are ready.*

I thought—maybe Anna, she said. *Maybe when she comes home.*

Yes, I said, encouraging her. *Anna will understand. She will know what to do.*

Nadia held out her hand and I took it. I kissed her fingers, the ring which made us husband and wife, and I told her I loved her. I told her we will do this together. I told her not to be afraid. I told her I would call from Prague.

Two days later, I arrived in the city and had been given orders to meet my partner—my access to the artist dissident underground—at a bar a few minutes from the Charles Bridge. The agent would wear a camel coat, drinking scotch in the middle of the afternoon. We were to attend a quiet going-away party for a dissident, where we would assist in their defection so we might uncover an artery into Europe.

Once my eyes adjusted to the dark, I saw that she was nearly as I remembered her. And there we were, only a couple minutes walk from where we had seen each other last. She looked over her shoulder at me and smiled.

Stepan, she greeted me, kissing my cheek. *Come, sit! Sit! A drink—a scotch for my darling cousin!*

So, we drank together. My name was Stepan. I wore civilian dress. I asked after her mother and father, my alleged aunt and uncle, and she performed well. Then it was time to go.

We'd better be off, she said. *Or we will be late.* Jara locked her arm in mine, and when we were out of ear-shot she whispered:

Aleksandr Ivanovich, how wonderful to see you again. We have a short walk, Mr. Ivanovich. Do you have anything to say?

No, I said. I felt cold toward her, irritated by her drunkenness. She stumbled a little on the cobbled streets in her heels. Prague was a labyrinth, and she led me into it. To where? We were supposed to be on the same side, and yet, when I met her years ago, she mourned her country. I thought of her as weak—I pitied her, despised her, thanks to my own guilt. And yet, I feared her.

As we neared the apartment, which she had pointed at with a slender hand, she stopped us and whispered, *You think I'm a traitor, Mr. Ivanovich. Better I died believing in my country than spying on them now. You think I'm a whore. You think I slept with you because I wanted to? You think I enjoy walking with you? You'll remember your captain, who told you to go with me—you'll remember his name was Chernov.*

They had my brother, a journalist. They had said he'd die or be sent to Siberia. He had been one of those keeping the Czech radio alive for weeks after the invasion. He said, you'll work for us, Jara Kučerova, or your brother will die. And so I worked for him, as a whore, as an informant. He told me to meet you on the bridge. You believe you were just an innocent boy? You think you were the first?

She laughed.

You think you're better than me, Aleksandr Ivanovich? Tell me, she said, her voice rising, breaking. *How am I not you?*

Here, she said, walking us forward again. *This is the street.*

She turned her back to me and knocked on the apartment door. The door opened and a woman answered.

Dear Jara, the woman said. *How wonderful!*

The woman—Vêra—took my jacket. Jara removed her camel coat, revealing a sleeveless green dress. She was striking.

We followed Vêra into the sitting room. A group of men smoked near the window, talking. The women sat together on the couch, legs crossed. They applauded Jara's entrance with kisses, squeezing her hand. Jara introduced me as her cousin while a handsome man approached me.

Stepan, he said. *Welcome. Jara speaks about nothing but you— ah, here she is.*

Jara kissed him on the cheek. *Milan,* she said. *Oh, how lovely it is to have us all together.*

Vêra joined us with drinks, and everyone came together around the coffee table. They were artists, musicians. Milan was a writer, his wife, Vêra, a former television announcer. The group was somber, feigned cheerfulness. It was Milan and Vêra's last day in Prague—the city of their childhood. Prague, where they fell in love and built a life. Their homeland. They would be emigrating, and Jara and I were ordered to plant a wire on Milan—the wire hidden inside my captain's cap, the battery in my pocket—while building connections with any other people of interest at the party.

It will be better in France, the group agreed.

A thin, pale painter said, *What life is it, for an artist in a communist state? Better to die remembered. Better to die free.*

Milan laughed. *Is it ever truly freedom if you are forced to leave your own country?*

Jara tipped her wine glass to her lips. She sat between Vêra and Milan, her knees turned against Milan's, her arm around Vêra.

No one dies freely, Jara said. She put the captain's cap on Vêra, and then laughed. The three of them, together, it was impossible to tell whose limb was whose as the cap was passed to Milan, to Vêra, to Jara. I drank the wine and watched them, an electric current circling, in waves. The others talked amongst themselves—some politics—but my focus was on Jara, who played two women at once.

I rose from my seat, feeling restless. The record ended, a Mancini record—how they managed it was a mystery. Not just a single record, but dozens. They had played it quietly, so no one could hear out the open window, which they had since closed.

What will we listen to, Stepan? Milan asked, rising to his feet beside me, looking at the records.

I wouldn't know where to start, I said. Feeling boyish from the wine, I said, *Everything. We can listen to it all.*

You just arrived from Leningrad, he said to me. *St. Petersburg. You're a pianist as well. So, you'd appreciate the symphony.*

Yes, I said.

I don't know if Jara has told you, but my father loved Stravinsky. I love Stravinsky. I despise how they treated him—the Russians. They loved their Tchaikovsky, but Stravinsky they destroyed, they disowned. Stravinsky also lived in France for a time.

I nodded in agreement. *An exile*, I said.

Yes, Milan said, grinning sadly. *He died in New York, just four years ago.*

I remember, I said. *I wonder if he wished he had died in St. Petersburg.*

I can't be sure, Milan said. *But he was rejected by his countrymen. I've been rejected by my countrymen. I know it's difficult.* There was a seriousness in the way he spoke.

I think Jara is right, I said. *It's the burden of life.*

Yes, Milan said. *But some of us must make a sacrifice.* He pulled from the shelf *The Rite of Spring*, and laid the record down, adjusting the needle on the groove.

The oboe rose like smoke and Milan left me as I leaned against the windowpane and closed my eyes. I thought of my own home. I thought of my own burdens. My own private life.

That night I drank. Jara watched me, uneasily. I was not working. I had so easily lost the will. The Czech had their ways of defeating me, of weakening me—with wine, with Stravinsky—and I suffered greatly. I closed my eyes and pictured Zoya, the way she would spin, wobbling like a top. She had wanted so dearly to be like her Aunt Anna, a ballerina like her mother, and they would instruct her:

Look for a point—look for a spot in the distance, and you'll never get off-balance. You'll never fall. And she'd spin once and stop. Spin and stop. The world tipping on its side and righting. Tipping, and righting. Again, again.

We lost a child but we were going to have another. I drank. I remembered. I forgot.

ON COMBUSTION

It was their dog, Dracula, who became sick first. Misha's mother made him beef and chicken mixed with rice.

Those first days, everyone was burned. They called it Acute Radiation Syndrome. Misha's skin itched, blistered. His mother had a bald spot on her skull that never filled. Vera's skin peeled, and she showed Misha the small sheets as they flaked from her body, the imprints of her pores and creases delicately pinched between her fingertips. Noticing loose tissue on her shoulder, Vera let Misha pull a flake off, and it was as if he were peeling back wrapping paper on a gift. He revealed the fresh skin underneath. Pink.

Dracula, his fur falling out, lying on his side. His pink tongue, spotted in black, dragging on the floor. He whined. He smelled of rot.

Misha's father carried the dog in a blanket to the woods. Dracula watched as Misha helped dig the hole. Misha kneeled to the shepherd, and Dracula licked his face. Misha kissed Dracula's crown. He stroked his ears. His father touched Misha's shoulder, and Misha, sobbing, ran away.

Before Maidan, Misha had only heard a gunshot once.

Misha lies in bed with Katya for the last time and tucks her hair behind her ear. She watches him. He can't look her in the eye.

"You'll go home," he says. "You'll see him again. And then you'll know."

She has been crying. He braves a smile. They make love slow. Everything moves slow. Except the sun, spiraling the days.

Misha wonders: *How much energy does it take to fuel the sun? To fuel a flower, a farm, a field? A power plant? How much energy does it take to mourn a father?*

How much energy does it take to light a candle in the church? Every day the first year after his father's death, his mother's hand, lifting, taking the match, striking it. His mother, saying a prayer for his father, and Misha, a boy, taking the match from his mother's cold fingers and lighting the candle, the wick a naked one, pure, unburned, white, and the sound it made when he lit it was surprisingly crisp, the licking of the flame surprisingly violent, the fire grew surprisingly fast.

How much energy does it take for the body to burn? His father was cremated after his death—his father's tall, angular body turned into ash in a porcelain urn, the urn glazed pearl-white like an eyeball. The round urn that once rested on the hearth, looking blind; Misha felt like it was following him everywhere he went. He avoided it, but always saw it—always felt it. The urn was eventually placed in a mausoleum, and Misha never saw the eye again; he felt both relieved and sad.

How much energy does it take to do wrong when you want to do good? To do good when you want to do wrong? How much energy does it take to die? How much energy does it take to live?

Katya folds into him. The sun rises. The day breaks. He feels afraid.

ODESA, UKRAINE
MARCH 2, 2014

Odesa is still on fire. Pro-Russian extremists and neo-Nazis call for the extermination of Ukrainians and Jews. Soon, pro-Russians will attempted to take the Odesa Regional State Administration building. Soon, someone will throw a hand grenade at a self-defence checkpoint outside the city.

Ka-boom.

And just like that, the war has arrived.

Slava attempts to avoid the news, so she has remained mostly in bed. She and her father have barely spoken, but he has brought her a small cake from the grocer. She had risen for a glass of water, saw the note with her name beside it. There was no written apology—he could only muster her name. She washes and begins to make them a stew for dinner. When her father returns, he winces when he sits in the dining chair, still scratches and bruises on his face from the strike with the rake. Her father eats little and drinks a little less, but only a little.

He asks, breaking the silence, "When will you leave?"

"Tomorrow morning. A friend will pick me up, and we will go to the airport."

He nods, drawing a spoon to his cracked lips. Her father is a hard man, fearsome. The epitome of a brute. And yet, how childlike he catches her gaze, flitting it away.

"Why come here?" he asks.

"I know now what it's like to lose someone you love and never hear from them again. What it does to a person. I just wanted you to know that I understand."

Her father's hand trembles, and he lifts the glass to his lips.

She will always forgive her father, because it was her father who found her, weeks after her mother had sold her. He had been lonely, seeking company. It was dark, the street wet and glowing in amber light. He was driving drunk when he saw her, his fourteen-year-old daughter, walking calmly toward the window of his car. She leaned into the window as she was taught to do. She said to him, trembling, "Mama—" in an effort to explain, and he said to her, "Get in the car, *koshka*."

He never raised a hand to her again—but he yelled, he threw glass, he broke a chair. Her father had become more fearsome than he had been before.

There was news not long after that the man who had taken her was dead. He was found shot dead, bloated in the sea.

Now, her father says to her, "You always knew what it was like to lose someone you loved. Long before you should have ever known."

It's when he says this that Slava feels unsure of leaving her father. Even when she had been bruised, she felt guilty, deserving. Even if he never said a word, even if he never asked her to stay, she felt afraid to leave him.

"Do you remember when you moved to Kyiv? Five, six years ago?" he asks her, as if reading her. Slava says nothing.

"I remember we had fought," he says. He puts down his fork and folds his arms on the table.

"I don't remember what about. I never remember. But the next day you were angry with me. You were still so young. You still are young. But you had packed your things, which was a very grown-up thing to do. And you said, *Tato, I am moving to Kyiv. I love you, but I can't be around you anymore.*

"I wanted to be angry. I wanted to tell you to go back to your room. But you were eighteen and already had that bag at your feet, and I knew it was done. I knew I could no longer stop it from happening. That you need a new beginning without the pain of this place. When I didn't say anything, you began to cry, and you hugged me. You said, *Just please be nice, Tato. Please.* And now, all the while, I realized how much you feared me."

Slava wipes her eyes with her hand. Her father reaches out to her. His hand is thinner, yellower, brittle. His bones wrap around her bones and his hands are cold.

"If your mother had been unhappy, she never said a word— not to me. But I never hurt a person until she left. Do you remember?"

Slava remembered a time when her father took her for ice cream. She remembers a pink dress. She remembers chocolate. She remembers the height of her father's shoulders. She remembers feeling like she could fall, and he would be a net. She remembers the smell of his cologne. She remembers the shortness of his hair.

It's the only nice memory she has of him. She doesn't tell him it's only one.

"I remember, Tato," she says. Her voice catches in her throat.

Slava goes from one side of the table to the other and holds her yellow father as he cries.

ON PAYING A DEBT

The summer of 2004, their first in Kyiv. Vera had earned positions teaching and performing violin, and Misha had interviews to teach at a university engineering department. It seemed impossible to Misha, the image of himself working in a clean suit, a sport jacket, when for so long he had labored alongside miners. He had been uncharacteristically engaged, invested, driven. In his private heart, it had pained him to leave the mines in Donestk.

But it was months after her mother's death that the collection notices arrived in Vera's name. Soon it became clear the debt Vera's mother had acquired. Gambling debts, credit, a significant portion of her life had been drifting on loans.

"It's unending," Vera said one night at the kitchen table, her hands covering her face. She had been unable to cry. The magnitude of the debt had for so long been unknown.

"Misha," she said, "what will we do?"

AUDIO CASSETTE RECORDING
SIDE TWO CONTINUED

Nearing midnight, the phone rang, and Vêra went to it. *Jara*, she said, grinning. *Pavol is on the phone.*

Can you keep track of all of your cousin's lovers? Milan asked me.

Impossible, I said, smiling at him.

Jara emerged, sullen. *Oh, he won't be coming after all*, she said. *He's upset with me—he'd forgotten where I was and called home, and mother was confused who he was. Apparently, she told him he's the flavor of the minute. I can't believe that woman.*

Jara turned to me, serious. *You must call her—my mother. She won't be angry with you. I told her you were with me, and she said she didn't believe a damn thing I say. Please, Stepan, call her?*

Calling Mother was code. The directorate had a message.

May I use your phone? I asked Milan and Vêra, and one of them showed me the way, back to the kitchen.

I dialed the number for Mother. It rang twice, then picked up.

Auntie, I said. *It's Stepan. Please don't be angry with Jara, you know how free-spirited and spritely she can be. I'm here, yes, at her friends'. Don't worry.*

I paused, the voice on the other end—a woman's—said, *You are to come home immediately, Stepan.*

Perhaps another hour? I protested. *We're having such a wonderful time.* It was impossible to leave without completing such a simple task.

She insisted.

Is it all right? Are you all right, Auntie? I had gained an audience. Jara stood next to me, concerned. We had been told we might expect a call if the place became hot, but we had been told we would leave together. We had to leave together.

No, the voice became stern. *Something's happened. I can't worry Jara. She's enjoying herself. But you—you must come home.*

The other line hung up. I lowered the receiver and looked again at Jara. It felt like a long moment, but we had to decide quickly.

I took my cap from the rack. I told the group I had to head to my aunt's, and their exaggerated cries of displeasure surprisingly warmed me, though I felt myself anxious to go. Jara ran to me, always an actress, and was now showing her concern.

She wants you to stay, I whispered to her. She shook her head.

We are supposed to leave together, she said. She looked sober, frightened.

I'm sure it's fine, I said. I wasn't sure. If the house had been hot, it was possible they were going to all be taken in. It was possible, with my arrival into the circle, Jara had become disposable. I went for my coat. She followed me.

Will you be back? she asked, arms crossed over her chest as if she were cold.

I don't know. I noticed her hand shaking. I took it. I slipped her the battery.

It's remarkable, I think, now, how much she relied on me in that moment. She was surrounded by her own countrymen, but it was I that she went to. Perhaps she didn't trust me so much as she feared me.

It's nearly done, I said. *Leave the device. Place it in the sofa, in the cushions. We can retrieve it later and try again.*

I took my cap and placed it on Jara's crown. A fraternal sentiment.

I will see you at home? I said loud enough for the others, who jeered me as I left.

When I arrived at the safehouse, Mother was there. She had curlers in her hair, smoking a cigarette over a cup of coffee at the small dining table.

Your wife is in the hospital, she told me before I could drop my bag, my coat.

I stared at her. I did not speak or move, as if doing so would condemn Nadia. I must have seemed to her an idiot. I looked at her, searching her, and she continued.

She tried to kill herself, she said, with the brusqueness of a doctor. *She isn't well. She's been put into a hospital. It was your sister who called. It's difficult, you understand, because you just arrived here. The Directorate is deciding now what to do.*

I said nothing. Understand it was better for me to not act desperate to get home.

Jara, I said. *The mission—*

If you're sent home, she will complete it without you. That being said, you'll likely be interrogated in Moscow. You understand?

She wouldn't do this, I said. *We were going to have a child. Another child.*

Mother looked at me a moment, and then down at her cigarette, which she snubbed.

You're sure? she asked.

Yes, I said.

The woman folded her hands together, looked off. She sighed. She felt around for another cigarette, offered me one.

Then, let's hope there will be no trouble, she said. She meant: let's hope I wasn't a spy. Let's hope my wife didn't try to kill herself to sabotage the mission, any mission. That my wife knew I was KGB. That I had told my wife everything of my work. Let's hope there was no conspiracy. Let's hope it was because she was ill, that she was only just gravely ill. Let's hope that this wasn't a political act. The Czech activist Jan Palach had lit himself on fire. And then there were others, as far as Ukraine, who self-immolated against the government.

But what Soviet citizen wouldn't want to live in the greatest nation on earth? My beloved's suicide was a crime against the State.

Mother and I. We smoked and waited.

When the door opened, it was Jara. We held each other's gaze with stoic relief.

It's done, Jara said. She handed me the cap. The wire was gone.

She joined us at the table, sitting next to me. Mother asked about the party, offering a smoke. Jara filled in the details, which I had forgotten as soon as she said them. The phone rang. Jara turned to me and whispered, *What's happened?*

Mother returned. She sagged in the lamplight.

You are to return to Moscow to care for your wife. You'll be gone less than a week.

She turned to Jara. *You will continue on tomorrow alone.*

Jara looked at Mother, and back to me, her face flushed, her hands still shaking, not with fear, but rage. I looked at my hands as she forced her way before me, turning her body into me, her body that smelled of sweat and perfume and booze.

Will you tell me what the hell has happened? Jara said. But I was tired of her.

Mother walked away and turned out the light in the hallway. When she had gone, Jara whispered again, and again, *Aleksandr? Aleksandr?*

I covered my face in my hands. I fell.

ON BECOMING A SOLDIER

It is the second of April. They sit in the garden alone. Misha kisses Katya's bare shoulder, her sweater having fallen. He has told her he is going back to Donetsk with the volunteer army, to fight against the pro-Russian separatists.

"I know families there," he says. "I feel like I need to go. Maybe there could be some good I could do. Maybe there will be less killing if I go."

When he looks at her, she does not waver, though she has started to cry. He reaches for her and she turns to him.

Katya says, "Misha, when will you learn? You can't save them. No matter how much you want to."

He pulls away from her. He leaves her and Katya calls after him: "You think I don't know? You think I don't fucking know what you feel?"

ODESA, UKRAINE
MARCH 3, 2014

Slava finds her father in his shed with a heater on, the orange cat curled on the workbench. He has a drink and lies on the cot on top of the wool blankets.

"You sleep here?" she asks.

"Every night since you left. The house is full of ghosts."

She thumbs the workbench. The cat, Morkva, lets her stroke his back.

"Why didn't you move?"

"No way of knowing if you'd ever come back."

She avoids his eyes and he says, "Don't look like that."

"I shouldn't have left."

"What's done is done," her father says. Slava nods. Morkva purrs. She doesn't know how to begin again.

"Whatever happened to him?" Slava asks.

"Who?"

"The man who took me."

Slava feels the chill, the fierceness of the cold. Her father smiles at her, the scars she's given him still open across his jaw.

"*Koshenya*," he says, pointing to her. "*Koshenya*," he says, pointing to Morkva. "Two kittens. Now, cats."

When she starts to speak, he says, "There's a car coming."

He tells her to make the guests the last of the tea before they leave. He tells her to travel safe. He kisses her forehead, a kindness she had long forgotten, and she opens her arms to him, tears streaming down her face, down her neck.

And when he lets her go, he begins to say *I'm sorry*, and the words fail him. Instead, she rescues him by promising, *I will be home again soon.*

The language of love is one without choice.
When we love, we say: *I fell in love.*
A trip. A stumble. A loss of balance.

Balance means evenness and harmony. Musicality. When we *fall in love*, we have been taken out of a state of balance and there is discord. We are taken off-guard. We are pushed into it, tripped, some would say. Some would say, *tricked.* Love is violent because we have been made a casualty from it.

The language of love is that which assumes a victim. Predator to prey. Cupid's arrow strikes a deadly blow. Love, an act of assault.

She stole my heart. He was blinded by love.
Kundera writes: *The physical act of love is impossible without violence.*

So, I've had three Great Loves:
My little sister, Anna, was my first.
Nedezdha, the second.
Jara, your mother, was third.

Since the USSR dismantled, I have been a piano teacher and piano tuner. Like a doctor, I carry a little satchel for making house calls to the instruments. Sick ones, out of tune and broken. Some keys dead.

Have you ever pressed down on a dead piano key? How empty it feels—like checking the pulse and finding it isn't there. You feel that silence before the skin cools under your fingertips. That silence. It is a hollowness that leaves you haunted.

I want to die. I am ready, now, to die. I have wanted to die many times. But not yet.

Not until I tell you.

Do you believe in God, dear Anna? I am not a religious man, but I served my country with the fervor of a priest.

That hollowness—when you pray, do you hear that silence? The silence that leaves you haunted? I've been driven mad by silence—by having too much, or not enough.

My piano teacher always told me I had poor timing. I hated the *rest*—those pauses before the music begins again. I hated the counting, the waiting, and he would tell me, *Aleksandr, breathe, breathe*, but I didn't know how long a breath to take.

How to measure the breath between notes? How then, to measure a life?

[A pause.]

Sergei Diaghilev, the Russian ballet impresario, when he heard the first notes of *The Rite of Spring*, said: *My God, how long does it go on like that?*

And Stravinsky, the madman, says: *Until the end, my dear.*

But imagine: A riot on the streets of Paris because of a Russian ballet. That bassoon rises like cigarette smoke from the orchestra pit, twisting like a spine, and the audience goes mad—

Only a Russian could do that. Only a Russian could make the whole world go mad.

I've known madness. I've seen it and felt it. The way it makes you feel like you're being put on trial. Everything is as real as it's not.

I wanted to be a soldier, but I didn't want to go to war. Still, a soldier has no choice. Being a soldier is a labor of love—love of country.

You were a child once, sweet Anna. I was a child once, too. Imagine your papa and Aunt Anna as children. I try to imagine my own papa as a boy. I cannot.

I thought I was a man when I was still a boy. There's that line from the Bible about becoming a man. Putting away childish things. I don't believe in God, but I believed I had reached that age—the age that makes you old enough to know things children shouldn't know.

War will teach you all sorts of things about yourself. It will tell you that you are a protector, a man of righteousness. War will tell you that you can do what you'd like, take what you'd like—a life, a woman, a nation. You take it because you can. You take it because you want to make it yours.

War will tell you, also, that you're made of blood and shit and that you can die as easy as a fly. Think of all the flies you've swatted dead. The ones you've killed on the windowpane near the stove because it lands in your hair, buzzes in your ear, sucks your food. All places you believe a fly shouldn't be allowed. So, you kill it, like that, without a second thought. When you kill a man maybe it could be the same way. When I die, I will be a fly—and I welcome it.

There are so many stories, dear one. So many stories to tell. Stories that outlive us, you and I—stories that can't be told in words. Stories that are impressed in our blood, like a map.

Why does a lion hunt the antelope?

Why does the Soviet stalk his enemy in the wood?

Because his blood compels him so.

ВІЙНА
WAR

Yea, and if some god shall wreck me in the wine-dark deep,
even so I will endure.
For already have I suffered full much,
and much have I toiled in perils of waves and war.
Let this be added to the tale of those.

—Odysseus, *The Odyssey*

THE HOUSE OF THE SUICIDE

It's in the middle of the night that she hears it, startling her from sleep. The rain is a mist, and his mother's house is shrouded in fog.

She goes to the living room, and the television is off, the light is on, the couch dented like a cast, but he isn't there.

She goes outside through the back door into the yard. She calls for Misha and the cold is a shock. She flashes a light and she can't see through the fog so she puts it away. She walks, her boots sucking in the mud in the garden, and she steps on something thick. She kneels and reaches toward the ground, feeling as if she were blind. She discovers with her fingertips a hand, the palm still warm.

Lying in the mud is Misha, a black bag over his head. The gun beside him.

Katya screams for help and kneels beside him in the dark, the fog, the wet earth. She can't stand—she slips on her hands and knees. Hair sticking to her face. She cries out and feels as if she's drowning.

Katya startles, waking from sleep. She hears the neighbors, riotous, and for a moment she forgets where she is, a nearby bang and crash quickening her heartbeat. Then she hears it, the familiar jeering, the celebratory bravado: Yankees lose. Katya goes to the window, comforted by the revelry, the laughter. A man separates briefly from his friends to throw a beer bottle into a tin trashcan, upsetting a gray tabby cat. Katya watches the man return to his friends. She watches the tabby as it runs.

DONETSK
SUMMER 2005

Oleg was waiting at a table for Misha with a well-dressed older man with a leather watch. Three vodkas were on the table. Oleg offered Misha a cigarette and lit the cigarettes for Misha and the rich man.

Oleg introduced him as Solokov—a man with an interest in mining in Donetsk. Solokov nodded and did not smile at Misha. Oleg's forehead was shiny, not from oil, but from perspiration. He wiped it away, but he did not seem nervous.

"Mr. Solokov is an important investor in Donetsk coal," Oleg said. "In Ukrainian coal. He has a series of projects across the area, which I am sure you've heard about from mining friends of yours."

Oleg leaned back in his chair, slowing his speech. "He has an interest in finding an individual to help him ensure the safety of his mining practices and workers—someone who can advise, also, about the safe transference of the coal. I mentioned you to him because of your hard work and excellent contribution to the Union, to our mines. In fact, we will need you to work both—though I have reached an agreement with Mr. Solokov to ensure you are not to be overworked and to spend as much time on his projects as he requires."

These rich men, oligarchs, making deals with the mafia, had been funding unregulated mines around Donetsk. Misha feared them. They funded men in power, men in the government, businessmen who took their cues from Russia. It was rumored President Yanukovych was involved, that he made money from the black-market businesses churning out illegal coal. Many men died working in them—but they were cheaper, and a way for coal to be harvested without governmental regulation and bought for low prices.

Legal coal, which needed to be enriched and graded, was expensive to produce. So, illegal unenriched coal was laundered into mines and sold as if it had been. In effect, Misha would become two sides on the same coin.

Oleg pressed. "It is important, Mikhail, that you do not discuss this meeting with anyone. It is more important than ever that you do not discuss this with your family, or anyone dear to you. You will be working closely with Mr. Solokov, with me, with very few others. It is dangerous work, and it is trying work, but you will be paid three times your typical salary. It is imperative you understand the importance for secrecy, for protecting Mr. Solokov, who will protect you, too. Do you understand, Mikhail?"

Misha leaned forward in his chair and touched his glass of vodka. He thought of Vera, who he loved, and his mother. He thought of his father—a good man. *How much energy does it take to be a good man?*

"I will need to travel regularly to Kyiv," Misha said. "To visit my wife."

Oleg grinned at Misha, taking a drag of his cigarette, crossing his legs. The rich man reached for his glass, then Misha, then Oleg. They raised their glasses, and they drank.

AUDIO CASSETTE RECORDING
SIDE TWO CONTINUED

There had been a note. When I arrived at the station I was greeted by two officers who took me in for questioning. There, they provided me with the letter written by Nadia.

I lost the baby, she said.

I can't lose another thing in this life, she said.

I'm sorry, Sasha, she said.

I love you, she said.

I was questioned. I was examined. After several hours, I was permitted to leave. They allowed me the letter. I folded it and put it in my breast pocket. It felt like a stone.

When can I speak to her? I asked. The officers looked at one another.

Comrade, the one said. *You are mistaken. Your wife is dead.*

So, they had finished it. I took my hat. I went home.

It was Anna I saw first in the garden. She had been waiting for me—she wanted to be the first to see me, I knew. She said nothing but wrapped her arms around my neck. Her heart to mine, between us, the letter from Nadia.

My Sasha, she said. *Dear Sasha.*

When she pulled away from me, she avoided my eyes.

Are they all inside? I asked.

Yes, she said. *Everyone. They're waiting to make arrangements.*

Waiting? I asked.

For you, Anna said.

I told her, *I have nothing to add. She was their daughter.*

Anna nodded. I asked her if they blamed me.

No, she said. *We all knew she was... we all knew she was...*

She didn't finish. I asked her, *Is there something else?*

Oh, Sasha. My dear sister seemed about to cry. *How transparent you make me.*

Well, I said. *Anna, what has happened?*

She picked leaves from a bush and cut them with her nails, severing the bits. The tips of her nails tinted green. She took my hand.

I go to New York in a few days, she said.

Yes, I said. *I remember.* She released my hand. Her palms had started to sweat.

She looked at the house, the door still closed. She wiped her hands on her skirt.

When I had gone before, I met someone. An American.

Anna, I said. *No more.*

She paced, she said it again and again, *You disapprove, I know.*

Anna, I said, finally. *No more.*

Your blessing, Sasha, she cried. *That's all.*

My sister was near tears. Her thin fingers covered her mouth as she feigned a cough. I pulled my sister's head to my chin, and I kissed her crown.

My Anna—Nadia's funeral was the last time I saw her.

My Nadia, it was the last time I saw her, too.

They dressed my wife in a mourning dress, black, without lace, the sleeves long, cuffing at the wrist. I wanted to touch her hand, turn her palm up, slide the sleeves above her wrist. Why hide what she had done?

I realize now how much we were asked to hide the parts of ourselves that were ugly. How often we were made to pretend. But the body feels pain before all else. The body remembers. And Nadia, even with her body covered, even with her casket open and her face upturned, I could see the lines of worry, the downcast turn of her lip. In death, my dear Nadia found no rest. I kissed her brow and erased the lines with my thumb. There was nothing more to be done.

I'm growing tired, now. There's so much I thought I had forgotten, that now in telling, I wish I never remembered.

[Indistinct.]

[Silence.]

[The sound of footsteps moving away.
The voice on the recorder distant, almost an echo.]

There's nothing for me here. I've not eaten in some days.
It is cold, and the young people have started singing at Maidan.
When I see them gathering on Khreshchatyk, I see the Czechoslovaks in Prague. When I see Prague, I see so much of my life that I wish to take back, to remedy, to cure.
Had I never left Moscow would Nadia have survived? No, I don't believe she would. She had decided when Zoya died that she wanted nothing more from life. It was because of me that she held on as long as she had. She longed to be gone years before. Yet, had I never returned to Prague, I would not have returned to Jara with immeasurable grief.

I arrived to the city early in the morning and met Jara at a café. She wore a blue dress. I remember I was glad to see her. Anna had gone, my wife was dead, and Jara was the only person familiar to me in a city not my own.

Good morning, she said.

We sat in some silence before I leaned over my coffee.

I'm sorry, I said to her.

She met my eyes.

I'm sorry, I said again, *for how that last night went. I know you were afraid.*

She nodded. *It's the nature of our work. I'm not owed anything. That's the way of it.*

I looked at my hands, near her hands. She was bold, unapologetic.

I'm sorry, I said, *also, for your brother. For what's happened to you and your family.*

With that, she had been stunned, or at the least, stirred. She crossed her arms and turned her face away. She said nothing.

I'm sorry that we have to work together. That this is the way of things.

She took out her purse and a pack of cigarettes. Without saying anything, she offered me one, and lit one for herself.

Is this a trick? she asked me.

No, I said. *I just lost my wife. My children are dead.*

What does that have to do with me?

I searched her. *It doesn't*, I said.

And yet, she said. *Here you are. Seeking compassion.*

She leaned over the table, into me. *You want to feel close to someone? You need trust for that. Let me tell you something while we're being honest with one another: the wire, it's gone. Not with Věra, not with Milan, or with any of their friends. I put it in a ceiling tile in the hallway of their building. I'm not a traitor.*

When I said nothing, she continued. She told me to tell my keeper, tell my officer, tell the directorate, that she was tired. She was tired of being a traitor. Her brother, her family—she was tired of officers promising her that her family is safe.

I dream at night that they're dead, Jara said. *I see them lined up like dolls, and then they're shot. Shoot me*, she said. She pleaded.

I said nothing to her. I took my coat.

When I got up to leave, she followed me, walked beside me. I walked toward the Charles Bridge and she kept pace. Neither of us spoke.

To the south of the bridge, on a column, is a statue of the Knight of Brunswick. He stands with a golden sword in his hands. I stopped at the column and turned to her.

This Duke of Bavaria—do you know the story? I asked her.

He was a pilgrim, she said. *The lion was loyal and followed him.*

My piano teacher, when I was a young boy, he told me this story. The knight finds himself in a wood, where he discovers a lion battling a dragon. He takes up arms and aligns with the lion. Together, they defeat the seven-headed dragon, and the lion and the knight remain side by side until death.

She looked at the statue. The morning air had a chill. It was the early days of spring. Her hair moved along her back.

I've thought about that lion a lot, returning here, I said. *When a young lion is exiled, when he comes of age, he has only one objective. He searches for a new pride.*

She turned from the knight to me. *What are you saying, Aleksandr Ivanovich?*

I'm saying, call me Sasha. I'm saying, you don't have to fight the dragon alone.

I don't know where it came from, that part of me. Perhaps the loss of Nadia changed me. Perhaps it was the ghost of my piano teacher, who had been a dissident.

Still, I hear my teacher's voice, asking me, *Sasha, what is Goodness? Is it God? Is it perfect? What is moral? Kant says: Goodness without qualification or judgement.*

My wife was dead. My children were dead. I felt myself, nearly dead, nearly alive.

In the Bible, Christ raises Lazarus from his tomb.

In April of 1975, Jara Kučerova smiled up at me while walking on the Charles Bridge.

BOSTON, UNITED STATES
April 4, 2014

Katya arrives at the café where Ezra is waiting. He has ordered her coffee, himself tea. She is sweating even though it is cold. She takes off her coat and hangs it on the back of her chair. She sits across from him.

He looks at her, his hands folded, hiding his mouth. He seems older, his eyes tired. He hasn't slept, she's realized. Neither has she.

"How was the flight?" he asks, as she adds sugar to her cup.

"Long," she says. "The layover in Prague was four hours."

He makes a noise of agreement, sympathy.

"I want to get right into it," she says, cupping her hands around her cup, the cup hot. "I've been sick thinking about it."

Ezra relaxes, leans back into his chair. "I thought you might." He smiles a little, but looks mostly sad.

She had written it out on the plane maybe thirteen different ways. There's something that changes it, makes it more real, when you say it aloud. There was no mistaking their mutual pain—the unrelenting heartache. For the first time since her son died, Katya was truly afraid.

"I didn't want it to be over," she says. "Up until I sat down. Maybe until I started speaking. I don't know what it means—whether it's irrational or not. I just feel it inside, and I don't think I knew how to feel it before. I don't think I knew how to listen."

She feels her throat tighten and she wants to say more, but it burns every part of her—the fear of it.

Ezra holds out his hand and she takes it.

"I love you," he says.

"I love you, too," she says. His thumb traces her knuckles. She realizes how much it is true. He squeezes her gently.

"It doesn't mean," she says, and she doesn't need to go on before Ezra nods.

"I know," he says. After a while, he seems sick. "I'm sorry, Katya. I'm sorry for what I've done."

"I know," she says. "I just want to heal. Every part of our lives has become broken."

Ezra nods. He asks her, "Where do we go from here?"

Katya says, "It depends where we want to go."

AUDIO CASSETTE RECORDING
SIDE TWO CONTINUED

What felt like years in Prague was only a matter of months. We planted wires, and yet only when we were alone did it feel like a crime. When the threat of death is on you, time is a dream. Jara and I worked the dissident circle, but we practiced a quiet rebellion. A quiet bending of glass.

I was still Stepan, her cousin, but in the safety of our home, when Mother was away, I called her my *kisa, my kitten.* No doubt we were recorded. No doubt. And though our work was thorough, in private we opened ourselves. An exhibition on the party line.

Why did you choose this line of work? she asked me. *The KGB.*

I realized Jara was the only woman who knew every side of me. She knew my work and my betrayal. Every aspect. I feared her as much as I loved her. And as she knew me, my love grew deep, along with my fear.

I wanted to be a good soldier, I said. *I wanted to believe in my country. Have you ever done anything, hoping to convince yourself of something?*

Yes, she said, curling into me. *I've trusted you.*

What are you trying to convince yourself of? I asked her.

That we will live a long life together.

I kissed the top of her head, along the hairline. I remember the smell of her. I remember her, the voice of her. I hear it and I don't hear it. I feel her and I cannot feel her.

Words are insufficient in telling this. Words are insufficient in relaying her. I can only tell you what happened. I can only tell you events, Anna. I wish I could give it to you, a piece of her, a moment with her. I wish I could give you more than I can— and isn't that the agony of it all? Never being able to say exactly what you mean. Never being able to say, *I loved her*, and have the world understand that, the weight of it, the way of it.

One night, Jara whispered in my ear, she wrapped her arms around my neck, and her voice shook—

I have your child inside me, she said.

Sasha, she said to me. *I do not want to die.*

You see, before, we had prepared ourselves. Every night we went to bed together, we knew we might not rise. I kissed her head and her hands.

What will we do, Sasha? she said, then. *Can we fix what we have done?*

Sweet kitten. Little lionheart. What does it mean to be a good citizen? What does it mean to be a good soldier? What does it mean to be a good parent? A partner? Is there objective goodness? A moral goodness? Like Darwin, do the different species of Goodness suck and suck in order to survive?

Jara and I decided we didn't care if we were good. We just wanted to survive. We wanted you to survive. Your mother and I decided that we would flee.

UKRAINIAN FILMMAKER OLEG SENTSOV ENDS 145-DAY HUNGER STRIKE IN RUSSIAN JAIL

FROM THE INDEPENDENT

OCTOBER 5, 2018

Oliver Carroll

After 145 days, Oleg Sentsov's lonely protest is coming to an end.

On Friday, the Crimean film director, controversially jailed by Russia on disputed terrorism charges in 2014, said he would be ending his hunger strike effective Saturday. In a handwritten statement released by his lawyer, he said he had been forced to abandon his protest because of the "critical state of his health" and the impending threat of hospitalization and force-feeding.

"Pathological changes have already started in my vital organs," the statement reads. "Force-feeding has been planned for me, and I have no say in the matter [...] In the current circumstances I am forced to end my hunger strike."

Valery Maksimenko, the deputy head of Russia's prison service, had earlier trailed Mr. Sentsov's announcement with a statement of his own to a state news agency. Mr. Sentsov had agreed to eat again, Mr. Maksimenko said, after being "persuaded by doctors... to choose life."

In his statement, Mr. Sentsov seemed to accept his protest had not had the effect he hoped for: "145 days of battle, 20kg less in weight, body destroyed, and the aim is not achieved," he said. "I'm grateful to everyone who supported me, and I ask forgiveness from those I've let down."

DONETSK, UKRAINE
AUTUMN 2007

Misha worked in six *kopanky* mines with thirty young men and five women dispersed throughout. The structures were supported by thatched-together wood beams. Misha had organized a small team to help him reinforce the structure of the mines above ground, and below.

The youngest woman was Petyr's sister, Yulia, who was only twenty-two and helped Misha as he searched the mines for weak beams, for rotting wood.

Yulia, who was intelligent and strong. Yulia, who was beautiful. Dark eyes and legs. She saved her money to go to the university. Yulia, who dreamed of being a nurse, mended the cuts and scratches that came from the work.

Misha and Yulia had been in the belly of a shallow mine. The ceiling was too low and the passageways were too narrow, and Misha had been working to find some way to expand the corridor of the mine without causing a collapse. He had recruited Yulia to assist him in adding a support beam to the weakened one, a process necessary for widening a passageway. They had on their helmets, respirators. The *kopanky* were not usually well ventilated, though Misha's team had also been working to deepen the mine, find cheap means to make it easier for the miners to work, to make it safer.

"It takes just as much energy to make a safe mine as it does to make an unsafe one," Misha regularly said to Yulia as they checked their gear before entering a mine. "Stay close."

Together with Yulia, Misha had created a map of the mines, labeled each beam, and used radios to communicate with miners as they worked. Misha's mines were the most advanced, he knew, of the illegal ones that the mafia monitored. He trained a few other engineers, but Misha's attention to detail was meticulous, organized, and superstitious. Men and women suffocated, died in the other mines. Solokov had asked Misha if he would like to have a better position, to manage more mines, to train a team of engineers—Misha had wanted to leave, to go home to his sick wife. Unable to say it, aware of his own snare, he said he liked being on the ground, he liked being in the mines himself, with the young people he hoped to protect.

Petyr and the other miners had gone up to the surface for air. Faces painted in coal, they ate their lunches in the shade.

Inside the mine, Yulia gently touched Misha's arm, examining a beam. The light from her helmet bright.

He thought of Vera. The last time he called she had been unable to speak. Yulia had given him such tender attention. But today, Yulia was bold.

When Yulia came behind him and slipped her hand under his shirt, up his back, they didn't hear right away. They didn't see it, when he turned to face her, and she kissed him, biting his lip, and his fingers tangled in her hair, his hands on her breasts, then her back. She tried to strip his shirt and she lost her balance, but when he corrected her, he leaned into a weak beam.

It was the beam that broke. It was the ceiling of the shallow mine that fell.

The air became thin and Yulia lay still but breathing. Misha could see the white teeth and the coal in her mouth.

Don't panic, Misha said. *Don't panic*, he said, his heart in his throat.

This is how I die, he thought. *This is how.*

Petyr and the others responded quickly.

They lifted Misha and Yulia from the choked earth.

It was only days later, while Misha was recovering, that he got the call from his mother. It went to voicemail; he had slept into the blinding afternoon. In his boxers, bruised and blue, he pressed play.

"Misha," his mother said. "It's time. You need to come say goodbye."

AUDIO CASSETTE RECORDING
SIDE TWO CONTINUED

I think of you often. I think of you every day. Not a moment passes where I have not thought of you.

Your mother told me she held you inside of her and her body became a shell. We packed light when we fled—just one suitcase between us—and she held her hand over her womb as we drove. She wasn't showing, but she wanted to comfort you. She wanted to keep you inside of her, safe so that you would bloom. She held my hand, and when the time came, she held her false papers, and I held mine.

We decided Greece because of the shore and because it was popular with emigres. In Greece, no one would know us. We wanted to raise you by the sea in the sunshine. Jara said she wanted to see the Temple of Athena. She wanted to seek the Oracle of Delphi. We found it on a map: the seaside town of Kirra, and so we started the drive from Prague to Yugoslavia.

As we neared the border, your mother did not flinch. She fanned herself in the heat. As we approached the border, we were asked for our papers. We had red passports—passports

I discovered from the homes of the dissidents we had wired. The border guard looked at my picture, then the papers. Jara fanned herself, smiled at another guard. I looked at the first guard, who looked at me, and I looked at Jara.

I remember it was a wet summer. I remember my hair sticking to my forehead. I remember the curling of Jara's hair at the nape of her neck, her hair tied up with a scarf. I remember the roses on the scarf were red. Her cotton shirt, blue. When I was asked to step out of the car, Jara caught my eye. I remember then, she did not look afraid. She looked as if she were ready to fight, to kill, to save you. She looked determined to survive.

I had gotten out of the car, my back wet from the vinyl seat, my legs chafed. I remember him and two others pushing me against the car. I remember Jara yelling, then her door slamming, and her screaming.

I remember seeing her, hate like a hurricane, screaming as they pinned her against the side of the car, in Russian, in Czech:

Ya beremenna—

jsem těhotná—

I'm pregnant, she says. *I'm pregnant—*

I began to fight back. After that, I forget.

I woke up in a dark room, light in my eyes, and your mother was gone. My body felt as though it was on fire, as if I had been dragged in the street. As if I'd been burned alive.

[Indistinct.]

A hard face, shadowed and severe, came into the light.

Aleksandr Ivanovich, he said to me. *I have many questions for you about your time in Czechoslovakia.*

He sat across from me, no baton in hand. He laced his fingers, leaned back comfortably. In the dark, I knew they waited.

But first, you must tell me: where has your sister gone?

EVOCATION OF THE ANCESTORS
PART I
SUNG BY KOBZARI

The Tatars took Slavic children of the Ottoman Empire and traded them as slaves.
The *Kozak* traveled to Kaffa on the Black Sea and freed the slaves. Two years later, they marched on to Muscovy.

Kozak is a criminal, a killer, a soldier. He robs, bribes. He is clever, brave. He changes sides.

Kozak protects Orthodoxy. He brings the printing press to Kyiv.
Kozak is a gypsy, dethroning sultans and kings.

Kozak fought for Poland and against Poland—
with Crimea and against Crimea—
for the Soviet and against the Soviet.

When the Soviet invades Ukraine, the *Kozak* carries his own flag. A stripe of red over a stripe of black. He hides in the woods. He travels in small packs. He shoots the Soviet and makes camp in caves.

When the Soviet discovers the *Kozak*, he kills his brothers and imprisons him.

When the German arrives, the *Kozak* makes a deal.

For protection against the Soviet, the *Kozak* decides again to kill the Jew.

AUDIO CASSETTE RECORDING
SIDE TWO CONTINUED

I will never know how they discovered us—the truth is that the pack is stronger than the lone beast. But I thought on it often, those early years in the labor camp, about the synchronicity of the timing, the pattern of events. I'd lie in fitful sleep and lucidly dream of being aboard a ship, no sun, no compass.

I recall the words of my teacher, the words of Zeus: *What a lamentable thing it is that men should blame the gods.*

Ah, ah. That's the error we make—not accepting our own lapses in judgment.

But—there is love, which is blinding.

And there is grace, which makes us see.

Anna had fled to the United States, escaping with an American lover after her final performance with the Bolshoi. The very night after her fateful act, I had fled Czechoslovakia with Jara. Had the timeline been reversed, perhaps Anna may have been the one captured.

Our parents died, orphaned from their traitorous children.

In the camp, I saw my father everywhere. In the barracks, the mine. I saw him in the stones and the rising dust. I saw him in the earthen world, etched in hardness, but I felt my mother on my shoulder. *Sasha*, she would say, *play for me—*

And I would hum for her. I would tap my fingers on my knees, and I would play.

Nadia and Zoya and the baby would visit me, in the snow. She'd leave footprints beside me, gift a flurry of snowflakes on my tongue. Zoya would make angels in the snow. The baby in Nadia's arms, blue, but smiling.

These ghosts kept me company as the months drifted that first year. A Ukrainian guard, a young, stocky *Kozak*, gave me news from the women's camp.

She's about to burst, he said to me when the snow melted. I shoveled the wet earth.

Any day now, he added.

I could not see him and shielded my eyes from the bright of the sun.

[Indistinct.]

Forgive me. This is a time I do not like to remember.

VIDEO RECORDING

It is night at Maidan. The men and boys are banging on trash cans and metal sheets, dressed in balaclavas and painted helmets. They laugh and sing. The babusi *fill their cups with hot tea and coffee. The women help others build a barricade, and there are a group of them, lifting the scaffold. There is a fire nearby. There is heavy smoke. A woman speaks to the crowd through a microphone, from the stage in the distance. A famous Ukrainian singer, she asks everyone to sing with her. They sing the anthem for Ukraine.*

It rises, the song does, and the men stop beating on the steel. You can hear the song rise while the men are building the barricade. Then they sing, too. They throw tires on steel and wood and sing the anthem of Ukraine.

Thou art not dead, Ukraine, see, thy glory's born again
And the skies, O brethren, upon us smile once more!
As in Springtime melts the snow, so shall melt away the foe
And we shall be masters in our own home.
Soul and body, yea, our all, offer we at freedom's call
We, whose forebears, and ourselves, proud Kozaks *are!*

The crowd cheers. The Ukrainian singer cheers, Slava Ukrayini, *she says.* Glory to Ukraine.
The scene cuts.
The scene opens.

It's Slava's apartment, the hallway. The sun is bright from the kitchen at the end of the hall. There is singing from the shower, the door cracked. The camera fogs as it nears the door, and Slava's voice is strong and loud. The sound of the water hits the curtain. Nothing can be seen—everything is heard.

Dascha says to her, her voice clear and close in the speaker—

That is the sound of my Yaroslava, *she says, laughing.* That is the sound of my love.

The scene cuts.
The scene opens.

AUDIO CASSETTE RECORDING
SIDE TWO CONTINUED

In Corinthians, the Apostle Paul wrote:

For now we see through a glass, darkly; but then face to face: now I know in part; but then shall I know even as also I am known.

What to say, now, to you? What to say. Have I seen you in Kyiv? Have I seen you? I wonder if you've looked through me. If I should see you, a woman now, would I recognize you? Could I see the curl of hair at the nape of your neck and know it was you?

In the camp, for fifteen years, I thought every instant of you, of your mother. We had been cursed at the start.

You were born in young April, dear Anna, under the planet Mars. You'll live by violence, you'll recognize it, and you'll know how fierce the act of love can be. The fury of it—how it wounds. And yet—we love anyway. We sacrifice all for love. Your aunt and I—we stood at the pyre and the whole world burned.

You were born in a labor camp, from a mother who survived great physical pain. The women surrounded her, I heard.

They held her hands and you came forward, sounding a cry. Your mother held you and an old midwife cut the umbilical cord. You learned to nurse at her breast. You learned how to breathe the air.

And when you turned one year old, the *Kozak* came to me and said, *Jara is unwell.*

And the next time he came to me, he delivered a note from her, which I opened in front of him. It said: *I love you. Save Anna.*

With a steady hand, the *Kozak* leveled me. I covered my eyes. How could I save you? How could I reach you?

It's the same question, all my life.

Abraham, for his love of God, offered up his only son.

He took the knife to slaughter, and the Lord God said, *Abraham, Abraham—Here I am.*

And the Lord God said: *I will provide.*

Anna. You, Anna. The Chosen One.

The *Kozak* took you from the labor camp. He would take you, he said, to his village. His daughter and son-in-law would take you as their only child. The *Kozak* said he would return, but he never did.

And this is how you were lost, little lioness. My dear kitten. This is how you disappeared.

THE ADORATION OF THE EARTH

In the morning, after he meets the woman on the train, after the play, after spending the night with Slava, Misha meets his mother at the cemetery, where he watches his wife buried. His mother walks ahead, a black scarf in her hair, and Misha trails behind. He is still drunk. The earth is wet. It smells of rain.

Misha turns back, looking toward the gravesite. Through the mist, he sees a tall but stooped old man, dressed in black, his back toward him. Misha thinks of stopping, of going to the man and asking how he knew her, his ethereal wife. Instead, he watches the man take off his hat and leave flowers on the grave, brilliant yellow. When the old man readies to go, Misha turns away.

Misha returns to the apartment he and Vera shared. The apartment where Vera died. He drops his bag and fumbles for his key. Outside the door is a package—an envelope. He drops the keys and tears it open. Vera's last cassette inside.

The envelope says, *For Misha. From: A. Ivanovich.*

THE DEATH OF ALEKSANDR IVANOVICH

Katya left Aleksandr, taking the phone number and cassette and putting it in her white coat near her heart. She went to wash her hands in the church, and then she stopped to watch a priest pray, blessing a hurt man lying on the floor. The priest spoke in Latin, or Greek, Katya was never sure which, but it sounded like a song.

She cried that night after Isaac had fallen asleep, as she walked the hospital to get some air, as Ezra had gone out to find them dinner. She saw a priest leave one of the rooms, and Katya stopped him, told him about her son, what Isaac had said, how she didn't know if she believed in God, that she was never a religious woman, and the priest said to her, "Come and let's pray," and so they went to the chapel in the hospital, and they knelt together, praying for Isaac and his health, praying for her heart, for Ezra's heart, that they might come closer to God, closer to one another through this all.

She left the chapel and thanked the priest, but when she looked at her phone, she had missed three calls—one from the hospital, two from Ezra—and she ran upstairs to Isaac's room, she couldn't wait for the elevator, and Ezra stopped her in the hallway because their son had stopped breathing and the doctors were doing all they could to bring his little heart back to life. Katya's own heart was pounding in her chest, in her head, and Ezra just kept asking her, shouting at her, *Where were you? Where were you, Katya? You were supposed to be with him—*

I was—she cried, but it didn't matter. Pushing him away, her strength surprising her, surprising him, the nurses at the desk stopped to look, and one came over to calm them both.

The doctor arrived, and it was like looking in a mirror—he didn't need to speak before Katya knew what he would say, because she had practiced it at home, in medical school, over and over again, *I'm sorry*, she said to her reflection in the mirror. *I'm sorry.*

I'm sorry, Isaac's doctor said.

After Aleksandr Ivanovich died, Katya called the number from his pocket again. She took the silver ring from his finger. She closed her eyes. *I'm sorry*, she practiced, whispering to herself, her throat tight from tears. *I'm so sorry.*

Please leave a message. She couldn't. Not then.

Beep, beep, beep, the phone said.

Beep, said Aleksandr's heart monitor. *Beep*, then nothing else.

LES AUGURES PRINTANIERS
THE AUGURS OF SPRING

This is a soldier, an orphan—then who should mourn?

—Yuriy Fedkovych

ILLEGAL RESIDENTS IN CHERNOBYL

like Misha's mother, are called *samosely*. In Ukrainian, it means, "self-settlers."

When Misha returned to Chernobyl after taking Katya back to Kyiv, when he told his mother that he would join the Ukrainian Army, Misha's mother doesn't protest, doesn't ask him to stay. His mother doesn't ask about Katya, she doesn't talk about Vera. She doesn't tell him, anymore, that she can't bear the thought. That the risk is too great.

Instead, she tells him a story of the *babushkas* who refused to leave their homes after the explosion in Chernobyl, a story that she had heard over and over again from the women that lived there.

"Shoot us and dig the grave," the *samosely* women said. "Otherwise, we're staying."

She kissed her son, hugged him, and with her rosary she said a prayer.

KOZAK II

When the Great War ended, Misha's father told him, tucking him into bed, a Soviet captain captured the *Kozak*. The captain allowed him water. He allowed him a last meal. The *Kozak's* hands and feet were secured to a chair that they brought to a clearing. He commanded his men to go back, to watch from the edge of the woods.

The captain equally admired and abhorred the man. He lit himself a cigarette. He cut the *Kozak's* hands free and offered the *Kozak* a cigarette. The captain braced his knee atop a boulder, facing the *Kozak*, and took the gun from his coat. The two men relaxed, smoking.

After a while, the captain asked the *Kozak*: *Tell me. You have no remorse for your crimes?*

The *Kozak* smiled. He said, *Ah, ah. What is a sin to the Devil? A prayer to God? What is Ukraine to a* Kozak? *To the Slav Tatar Pole German Russian Jew? My country is an open wound. My country is red blood on black earth. I ask you: What would a captain do for the love of his men? What would a captain do for the love of his country?*

The *Kozak* flicked the hot ember into the brush around his chair, between himself and the captain, his feet still tied. The captain fell back. His men ran to the camp for water, but the fire was immediate. The swell was remarkable and final.

The *Kozak* shouted from the hell-flame at the captain, at every one of us all:

Tell me, Comrade! How am I not you?

PRIPYAT, UKRAINE
AUTUMN 2007

Misha wasn't working when the Zasyadko mine collapsed and killed one hundred men inside. He wasn't in Donetsk when he read that Solokov fell from his penthouse apartment after the disaster. Some news said it was an accident, but there are no accidents in Ukraine. Just consequences.

He had gotten the call from Oleg that many government workers would be fired. Misha was already on leave in Kyiv.

"It's time," his mother said, then. "The whole world is hell."

So, they packed her things and went to Pripyat. At the gate the border guard stopped them. When he took their papers, the guard said, "Misha Tkachenko. You bastard." He laughed.

Petyr had worked in the Solokov *kopanky* mines for years before Misha had arrived. It was rare that Misha would see his face clear of coal. Like Misha, he received threats if he left the mines. Unlike Misha, Petyr had the muscle of a gang behind him—the type of organized criminals able to allow him to leave the mines and give him access to Chernobyl.

Now, he had grown a beard.

"You've heard the news?" Petyr asked. He meant, *Did you hear? Solokov is dead.* "You're better off now, my friend."

Petyr opened the gate, letting them pass. It was Petyr that checked on his mother while Misha was away.

Seven years later, while Katya made jam with his mother in her garden, it was Petyr who said to Misha, walking in the woods of Chernobyl, "I'm going to go fight, lead a battalion. Yulia has gone off already with the Donetsk People's Republic."

"Come with us," Petyr said. "It will be as old times."

Misha shakes his head and says to him, "You will always be my brother, Petyr. But on this, I must go the other way."

Petyr holds out his hand, and Misha shakes it.

Misha says to him, "Be safe, brother. Tell Yulia to be safe, too."

It was Petyr who would fight for Russia. It was Misha who would fight for Ukraine.

THE WAR IN DONBASS
SUNG BY KOBZARI

Ukrainian fights Ukrainian for Ukraine.
Men and women fight men and women, brothers and sisters,
two halves, the rib of Adam plucked like a wishbone: two parts
from a whole.

An apple split to the core, the seeds spreading, a seed sprinkled in coal.

Ukraine, made of East, made of West
like the sun cycle for the day,
like the moon cycle for the night,
the land spiraling in-between.

Time is a circle. At the center of the circle is the core.
In the core of the apple seed, there is arsenic.

Ukraine is at war, but the world doesn't yet call it war.

*First there was the Word, and the Word was with God, and the
Word was God.*
Adam named the beasts in the Garden of Eden, and that is what
they were called.

Call something by its name, and it becomes it.
It becomes what it is, it becomes owned.

Things, they say, come in threes:

Eve, when she encountered the fruit, experienced three
aspects of Temptation:
That it was good for food,
A delight for the eyes,
And the tree was to be desired to make one wise.

Christ, too, was tempted three times:
The Devil tempted him with bread,
To prove he was the Son of God,
To take the kingdoms of the World.

In Ukraine there are three modern cries for freedom:
First, there is the Ukrainian freedom referendum.
Then, there is the Orange Revolution.
Then, there is Euromaidan.

When the war begins in Donbass, there are two tries for peace:
First, there is the Minsk Protocol.
Then, there is Minsk II.
Still, there is no ceasefire, there is no peace.

For a long time,
The West calls it a *conflict.*
Ukrainians say:

Ah, ah.

Oh, my friend.
We have seen it all before.

DONETSK AIRPORT
MAY 26, 2014

A soldier near Misha was shot from separatist fire, shot near the eye, in the skull, and his head falls onto his shoulder, his grip loosening around his gun. Misha takes his ammunition, and ducks behind a barrier inside the airport, what's left of it, and with two other soldiers, Andrushkiv and Hycha, the three cover one another as they search for a stairwell to restock, to find a reprieve from the gunfire.

It's only when the shelling stops that there's danger.

The Donetsk People's Republic, the DPR, the separatists, have destroyed the terminal—the building looks skeletal, remnants of steel, wires, glass, concrete have been piled around the Ukrainian Army, pouring around them like rubble, the building less a building and more like something organic, something constantly changing, less alive, though, and more decomposing—a creature, dying.

Andrushkiv yells, *Move,* and so they go.

Outside, the DPR had collapsed the air traffic control tower, shelling it until it fell, a plume of dust swallowing it, the men inside the tower falling, dropped as if they were toys.

It is May 2014, though Misha is not exactly sure which day.

Before he left Pripyat, he listened to a cassette that he returned to often—the last one Vera recorded before she became sick, the one left for him at the door to their apartment in Kyiv after her funeral. She played off-key. She had, even then, become terribly weak. But the song, she says on the recording, her voice ethereal before she plays, *is supposed to be this way.*

Here—Hycha says. There is one dead man, DPR. It is not Petyr, and Misha is relieved.

The Army has, in the last few days, recaptured the airport from the DPR, though many men have gone missing, have been taken, have been killed.

The shelling stops.

Cover—

Tank fire blasts the terminal. The ceiling above them falls on Misha and his men beside him, and Misha is partially buried, blinded. He cries out but his brothers are silent. Dust fills his mouth. Then he feels it—the most magnificent weight.

Two soldiers arrive, both women. They are charged with taking prisoners of war and leading fallen men to safety. They lift away the ceiling rubble, dragging bodies into the dead grass, the dirt, calling out to one another in Russian.

This one is alive, one woman said.

The second woman comes closer. The woman's hands touch his face, inspecting him, and she takes off his helmet. They recognize one another. Yulia, no longer a girl in a coalmine, screams for help.

Misha, hold on, she tells him, trembling. Bratishka, hold on. She is ready to leave for help.

He reaches for her and Yulia kneels beside him.

Stay with me, he says to her in Russian. She holds his hand.

PASSENGER AND CREW MANIFEST READ ALOUD AT TRIAL FOR VICTIMS OF MALAYSIAN AIRLINES FLIGHT MH17 FROM AMSTERDAM TO KUALA LUMPUR

PASSENGERS

John Adler
Christopher Allen
Ian Allen
John Allen
Julian Allen
Stephen Leslie Anderson
Andre Anghel
Mabel Anthonysamy
Ithamar Avnon
Robert Ayley
Joyce Baay
Theresa Baker
Wayne Baker
Willem Bakker
Rowen Bats

Emma Bell
Natashja Binda
Muhammad Afruz Bintambi
Muhammad Afzal Bintambi
Marsha Azmeena Bintitambi
Helen Borgsteede
Catharina Bras
Wilhelmina Louise Broghammer
Therese Brouwer
Elisabeth Brouwers
Anton Camfferman
Benoit Chardome
Carol Clancy
Michael Clancy
Regis Crolla

Edith Cuijpers
Auke Dalstra
Cameron Dalziel
Minh Chau Dang
Quoc Duy Dang
Francesca Davison
Liam Davison
Elsemiek Deborst
Barbara Maria Debruin
Johanna Dehaan
Annetje de Jong
Pim Wilhelm de Kuijer
Saskia de Leeuw
Liliane Derden
Esther de Ridder
Joop Albert de Roo
Christiene de Sadeleer
Maria Adriana de Schutter
Maarten Devos
Aafke de Vries
Shaliza Zaini Dewa
Esther de Waal
Donny Toekiran Djodikromo
Fatima Dyczynski
Lisanne Laura Engels
Tamara Ernst
Emma Essers
Peter Essers
Valentijn Essers
Shun Po Fan
Ming Lee Foo
Bryce Fredriksz
Ariza Binti Gazalee
Angelique Gianotten

Kaela Maya Jay Goes
Paul Goes
Marco Grippeling
Wilhelmus Grootscholten
Jill Helen Guard
Roger Watson Guard
Darryl Gunawan
Hadiono Gunawan
Irene Gunawan
Sherryl Gunawan
Anne Mieke Hakse
Davy Joseph Gerardus
Megan Hally
Yuli Hastini
Geertruida Heemskerk
Lidwina Heerkens
Robin Hemelrijk
Susan Hijmans
Andrew Hoare
Friso Hoare
Jasper Hoare
Katharina Hoonakker
Howard Horder
Susan Horder
Astrid Hornikx
Pieter Jan Willem Huijbers
Arnoud Huizen
Yelena Clarice Huizen
Maria Huntjens
Olga Ioppa
Cornelia Janssen
Kevin Jesurun
Rishi Jhinkoe
Tambi Bin Jiee

Subashni Jretnam
Mattheus "Theo" Kamsma
Qiu Qing "Guo" Kamsma
Yvonne Kappen
Vickiline Kurniati Kardia
Karamjit Singh Karnail Singh
Karlijn Keijzer
Barry Kooijmans
Isa Kooijmans
Mira Kooijmans
Oscar Kotte
Remco Kotte
Hendrik Rokus Kroon
Johannes Lahaye
Gerda Leliana Lahenda
Hubertus Lambregts
Joseph Lange
Gabriele Lauschet
Jian Han Benjamin Lee
Kiah Yeen Lee
Mona Cheng Sim Lee
Why Keong Lee
Yau Chee Liew
Yanhwa Loh
Henricus Maas
Edel Mahady
Emiel Mahler
Lisa Marckelbach
Elizabeth Martens
Sandra Martens
Evie Coco Anne Maslin
Mo Robert Anderson Maslin
Otis Samuel Frederick Maslin
Tina Pauline Mastenbroek

Richard Mayne
Mohd Ali Bin Md Salim
Ingrid Meijer
Sascha Meijer
Gerardus Menke
Mary Menke
Hannah Sophia Meuleman
Anelene Rostijem Misran
Augustinus Moors
Meling Anak Mula
Johanna Nelissen
Elisabeth Ng Lye Ti
Ng Qing Zheng
Ng Shi Ing
Ngoc Minh Nguyen
Tim Nieburg
Dafne Nieveen
Tallander Franciscus Niewold
Rahimmah Noor
Jan Noreilde
Steven Noreilde
Nicoll Charles Anderson Norris
Jolette Nuesink
Jack Samuel O'Brien
Daisy Oehlers
Victor Oreshkin
Julian Ottochian
Sergio Ottochian
Lubberta Palm
Miguel G Panduwinata
Shaka T Panduwinata
Hasni Hardi Bin Parlan
Johnny Paulissen
Martin Paulissen

Sri Paulissen

Sjors Adrianus Pijnenburg

Alex Ploeg

Robert Ploeg

Benjamin Pocock

Kaushalya Jairamdas Datin Punjabi

Hielkje Raap

Jeroen Renkers

Tim Renkers

Daisy Risah

Albert Rizk

Maree Rizk

Catharina Ruijter

Arjen Ryder

Yvonne Ryder

Quinn Schansman

Cornelis Schilder

Rik Schuyesmans

Hendry Se

Helena Sidelik

Siti Amirah Parawira

Matthew Ezekial Sivagnanam

Paul Rajasingam Sivagnanam

Gary Slok

Carlijn Smallenburg

Charles Smallenburg

Werther Smallenburg

Maria Smolders

Jane M Adi Soetjipto

Peter Souren

Reinmar Specken

Cornelia Stuiver

Wayan Sujana

Supartini

Liam Sweeney

Muhammad Afif Bin Tambi

Charles Eliza David Tamtelahitu

Siew Poh Tan

Elaine Teoh

Yodricunda Theistiasih

Glenn Raymond Thomas

Mary Tiernan

Gerardus Timmers

Cornelia Tol

Hendrik Jan Tournier

Liv Trugg

Remco Trugg

Tess Trugg

Thamsanqa Uijterlinde

Lorenzo van de Kraats

Robert Jan van de Kraats

Jeroen van de Mortel

Milia van de Mortel

Johannes Rudolfus van den Hende

Margaux Larissa van den Hende

Marnix Reduan van den Hende

Piers Adnan van den Hende

Christina Anna Elisa
    van den Schoor

Laurens van der Graaff

Jennifer van der Leij

Mark van der Linde

Merel van der Linde

Robert van der Linde

Bente van der Meer

Fleur van der Meer

Sophie van der Meer

Ericus van der Poel

Paulus van der Sande
Steven van der Sande
Tessa van der Sande
Inge van der Sar
Jan van der Steen
Frank van der Weide
April van Doorn
Caroline van Doorn
Gijsbert van Duijn
Petronella van Eldijk
Rene van Geene
Erik Peter van Heijningen
Zeger van Heijningen
Allard van Keulen
Jeroen van Keulen
Robert van Keulen
Petra van Langeveld
Klaas Willem van Luik
Lucie Paula Maria van Mens
Adinda Larasati Putri van Muijlwijk
Emile van Muijlwijk
Stefan van Nielen
Jacqueline van Tongeren
Anthonius van Veldhuizen
Pijke van Veldhuizen
Quint van Veldhuizen
Huub van Vreeswijk
Winneke van Wiggen
Frederique van Zijtveld
Robert-Jan van Zijtveld
Kim Elisa Petronella ver Haegh
Marie ver Meulen
Erik Vleesenbeek
Cornelia Voorham

Wouter Vorsselman
Eline Vranckx
Hendrik Wagemans
Amel Wals
Brett Wals
Jeroen Wals
Jinte Wals
Solenn Wals
Leonardus Wels
Sem Wels
Ineke Westerveld
Ketut Wiartini
Marit Witteveen
Willem Witteveen
Ninik Yuriani
Desiree Zantkuijl

FLIGHT CREW

Wan Amran Bin Wan Hussin, Captain
Eugene Choo Jin Leong, Captain
Ahmad Hakimi Bin Hanapi, First Officer
Muhamad Firdaus Bin Abdul Rahim, First Officer
Mohd Ghafar Bin Abu Bakar, In-Flight Supervisor
Dora Shahila Binti Kassim, Chief Stewardess
Azrina Binti Yakob, Chief Stewardess
Lee Hui Pin, Leading Stewardess
Mastura Binti Mustafa, Leading Stewardess
Chong Yee Pheng, Flight Stewardess
Shaikh Mohd Noor Bin Mahmood, Flight Steward
Sanjid Singh Sandhu, Flight Steward
Hamfazlin Sham Binti Mohamedarifin, Flight Stewardess
Nur Shazana Binti Mohamed Salleh, Flight Stewardess
Angeline Premila Rajandaran, Flight Stewardess

AUDIO CASSETTE RECORDING
SIDE TWO CONTINUED

In 1991, my country split apart. The borders fell open, and so did the prison.

I was released, but I was not free.

[A pause.]

What happens to an old soldier, without a war to fight?

What happens to an old man, without a country?

I looked for her—

I looked for you—

Jara. She had been limitless. Having never seen her grave, my child, I still dream she is alive. Just as I dream of you. I went to Ukraine to find the *Kozak*, to find you.

I taught the piano to children. Boys and girls once my age.

At night, I play in the streets of Maidan.

[Silence. The sound of a chair, creaking.]

I repaired the instruments as I always had, but it was only after prison that it seemed I learned to understand them. I searched each piano for the voice.

I waited for it to instruct me.

I waited, and then it sang.

It said to me, *Freedom, Aleksandr Ivanovich, is the state of being at peace with oneself.*

I worked for many years until I met her—a woman I was certain could have been you, could have been a mirror of your Aunt Anna. She would have been your age, then. She saw my advert in the paper, and she called. She told me she knew how to play, but she wanted to learn more. I also suspect she was in search of company. As was I.

Her voice was warm. I liked the tenor of her laugh. I went to her home while her husband was away working in the mines in Donetsk. We started our lessons and she kept a cassette recorder atop the piano while she played. She insisted on keeping it on, throughout our modifications and corrections. I tried to stay mostly quiet, feeling only truly comfortable around her when she turned the tape off.

She said it was for her husband. She said, *We often miss one another and can't talk on the phone. I send him these instead, like little letters. I talk to him for hours, sometimes. Sometimes I just let it record while I listen to music, or practice. He says he loves them. He waits for them every week.*

I remembered all the pianos and dens in Prague where I had once planted recording devices, where stranger would listen to stranger. The erasure of privacy. But this was its opposite. It was intimate, special.

She must have seen me thinking it through, because she said to me, *Perhaps you would like to share your story.*

At the time, I shook my head. I said, *No, no.*

But one afternoon I sat beside her on the bench of the upright. I remember the sun was hot on the oak. She had come to my apartment and I had put on some tea. She looked paler, thinner than I last remembered.

Her name was Vera. Vera, like the Latin *verus*, meaning True, or Faithful.

Vera turned to me, her eyes meeting mine, and said: *I'm dying, Aleksandr.*

I realized, then, that she, like me, was a maimed animal, circling in its cage.

We played until she couldn't. She would get tired earlier and earlier, and after a while I stopped teaching her altogether. I would visit her and her mother-in-law, and when the mother had gone out, Vera would say to me, *Tell me a story, Aleksandr.*

I told her everything, everything I've longed to tell you. She tried to find you—she worked so hard on that, her little computer on her lap in her bed. She found a phone number, a number I never dared to call because I was afraid it wasn't correct. She begged me to try, but I couldn't bear it. I promised her one day I would. But for now, I carry it with me. I carry it now, in my pocket. A little bit of Vera. A last little bit of hope.

Shortly before she passed, Vera also left me her recorder, and a blank cassette. She had already written on the tape: *For Anna.*

ON LEAVING HER HOMELAND

Slava sits beside the window on the flight to Los Angeles. Alexis takes the aisle, leaving a seat between them. She locks their carry-ons above, clicking the latch into place, her blond hair bright like white. When the plane begins to move, Slava tenses and grips the armrests. Her heart thunders. Her stomach knots. Waifish Alexis senses her fear and touches Slava's knee.

"Don't worry," she says. She offers her hand and Slava takes it. Slava closes her eyes.

The plane taxis. Slava remembers her countless trips on the train, the subway in Kyiv. She remembers the ferries and the boats in Odesa. She remembers when he took her—the son of her mother's friend—when he lied to her and told her she would be safe. He took her bag, her money, her clothes. He said to her, *You work for us, now.*

Please, she had said. *Please take me home.*

I was fourteen, she said to Adam, recording her. *I worked six blocks from my father's house.*

The engines roar, and her heart becomes her stomach. She remembers all the times she ran from home—from her father. She remembers running from Maidan, to the church.

She thinks of Misha, who she could not find a number for, so she called the doctor, Katya, who she met in the church. She called her at the terminal and said, *Come see me in L.A.*

The plane tips—

Alexis says to her, "Look, Slava—look!"

And Slava can see it—her whole country, both vast and small.

She looks out the window at the land and the rivers and the sea and her father and her mother and Dascha and Misha and Maidan until they disappear beneath the fog of white.

Slava closes her eyes and she feels herself lift.

PETRO POROSHENKO ELECTED NEW PRESIDENT OF UKRAINE
MAY 25, 2014

In the wake of civil unrest, former Ukrainian President Viktor Yanukovych left Kyiv last February to seek asylum in Moscow, where he was greeted by the Kremlin and President Vladimir Putin.

Elections in Ukraine had been scheduled for March 2015, but were pushed early in order to establish new leadership in a country reeling from a four-month revolution, which began in November of last year. Mr. Poroshenko won the election in the first round of votes, taking 54.7%, followed by Yulia Tymoshenko, who won 12.81%.

Sixty percent of voters participated in the election, as cited by the Central Election Commission—however, that does not include regions in Ukraine that are not currently under governmental control. Crimea, which has been illegally annexed to Russia, did not hold elections. In conflict regions of Eastern Ukraine, particularly Donetsk and Luhansk, voter turnout was greatly inhibited by extremist groups, with only twenty percent of the population voting.

Many difficulties lie ahead for Mr. Poroshenko, who will be inheriting a fragmented and war-torn Ukraine.

THE RESURRECTION
OF ALEKSANDR IVANOVICH

It's after the labor camp that Aleksandr Ivanovich finally returns to Moscow. He arrives at the home of his parents—his childhood home. His mother and father are long gone, he's known now for a while. But it is the faded wallpaper, the broken glass, the ruined portraits that cause him to weep.

Much of the home has been destroyed, items taken. The old black piano stands in the corner along the wall, and he longs for his teacher.

Aleksandr opens the piano as he had as a boy and sees the parts where it had been broken. He plays the dead keys, noting which ones require tuning. It's under the hood of the piano that he feels the familiar numbers etched in the wood, the serial number he tried his whole boyhood to remember. It's there that he sees the small envelope taped to the inner shell, as if it were inside a ribcage. It's addressed *To A*.

Inside is a silver ring—his father's wedding ring.

The note says:

Mother's ring was taken. I leave you mine. Anna is gone and so soon we will be. I have no anger, no fear. I feel only tremendous loss. Find Anna. Protect her. Love—Papa

And so, his father did not yet know of his son's own betrayal, of the labor camp, of the years his own son lost. At the time of this note, he may have not known—but he gave him permission. Permission to leave.

Aleksandr finds in his parents' bedroom his father's uniform. He is too thin for it, so he puts the coat over his own. The jacket is decorated handsomely. If it wasn't for the dust, for the glass, for the broken picture frames, the overturned dresser and akimbo drawers, for the ripped fabric and the smell of rat—he may have admired it longer.

Before he leaves Moscow, Aleksandr puts an ad in the paper for a truck and a few men. He will take the piano with him, he decides. He will take the piano with him to Kyiv.

ON FLIGHT

Vera hated it—she hated that her husband worked in a mine, that he only came home four days a month, coal under his fingernails.

"This is what we need to do," Misha said. "Just for now."

"This is not what I imagined our life to be like," she'd say, sitting at her mother's old piano.

Misha remembers thinking, *When Solokov's work is over, we could have a child.* But Vera wanted to try, anyway. The child never came.

At first, trying was a joy, exciting, a release. But each month came and went, and then after nine months of trying she began to worry.

"What's wrong with me?" she'd say, blood between her legs.

"It's not you," Misha would say. "It's not you. I will go to the doctor." But he was afraid.

When the doctor told Misha his sperm count was fine, he said, "Your wife may need to make an appointment," writing with a pen. "We will take a look at her health. Then we can discuss options."

Vera, who hadn't gotten out of bed that day, who had been having trouble eating, stirred to see him. Vera looked at the ceiling, her face thin and white. Misha drew her to him.

"I feel as if I've lost all sense of feeling," she said. "It's the strangest thing."

A week later, Vera went to see the doctor, who took samples from her, who looked inside of her. The doctor inspected her body, her breasts, her uterus, and when she touched Vera's throat, she felt a mass.

Misha had returned home, knowing it was urgent. The picture was on the table.

"It looks like it's mid-flight," said Vera, looking at the moth image. A Rorschach.

"Maybe it'll just fly away," she whispered into his ear, squeezing his hand.

SAMOSELY

MAY 2014

She is in the garden when she sees him—a man in military fatigues. He approaches the edge of her garden, the fruit and vegetables ripe and full. She has finished canning and jarring for the day. Now, she pulls the dead, dry stalks from the earth. She squints into the sunlight and lifts the brim of her wide hat to greet the visitor.

He removes his cap politely and says, *Good afternoon, babusya.*

It was days ago when she had the feeling—sitting at the dining table. A chill at the open window from a stray breeze, disturbing the warmth within the house. She heard them: her husband's voice and her eager son. She felt the dog kick between her legs. She closed her eyes and listened to her son ask about the frogs in the river—how they grow from tadpoles to having legs. Her husband holds a book with drawings, showing how they change.

She had opened her eyes, startled. She was alone again. Outside the window: the chirp of frogs singing. She realized it then.

Now, the old woman looks at the soldier at her fence. He opens his mouth to speak and she waves her hands to gently quiet him.

Come, she says to the soldier, *come inside, dear. I will set the kettle. Then, we will talk of what's to be done about my son.*

AUDIO CASSETTE RECORDING FOR MISHA, FROM A. IVANOVICH

[Vera, laughing.]

Are you ready?— [Aleksandr Ivanovich laughs.] What would you like to say?

To my husband Misha—I love you more than anything. Now, your turn.

No, no.

Oh, come now, Sasha.

First, we play.

МЕСЕНДЖЕР
MESSENGER

It is a wise child who knows his own father.

—Telemachus, *The Odyssey*

EVOCATION OF THE ANCESTORS
PART II
SUNG BY KOBZARI

Mykhailo Hrushevsky, the pre-eminent historian of Ukraine, died in exile in Kislovodsk, Russia.

Taras Shevchenko, Ukrainian poet, artist, and activist was buried in St. Petersburg. His friends recovered his body and took his remains by horse and train to a hilltop and reburied him above the River Dnieper.

A Heavenly Hundred died in Kyiv. Thirteen thousand from the war in Donetsk. Two hundred and ninety-eight on a crashed Malaysia Airlines flight. A million by Gulag. Ten million by starvation. One hundred twenty thousand murdered Jewish Poles in L'viv.

The land, ripe with coal and wheat, is also rich with blood.

ON SEPTEMBER 7, 2019
FILMMAKER OLEG SENTSOV

returned safely to Kyiv, Ukraine, as one of thirty-five Ukrainian citizens released in a prisoner swap with Russia. He was greeted by his daughter and welcomed by President Volodymyr Zelenskiy.

The filmmaker said in a recent press conference, on whether Russia is considering peace with Ukraine:

"Even the wolf wearing sheep's clothing has his teeth sharp. Don't believe it. I don't."

LOS ANGELES, UNITED STATES
JULY 2014

Slava has been living in Los Angeles for nearly four months now. She has started running before the sun rises, hair long enough to tie back. She has started formal lessons in English, which she enjoys. Slava has moved into the spare room in Alexis and her girlfriend's apartment. The girlfriend is named River; her hair is knotted in dreadlocks, and though she does not speak Ukrainian or Russian, Slava simply enjoys her steadying presence, the smell of incense, the sound of her guitar.

There is a war happening in Ukraine, but Slava is eager to return, even for a few weeks. Adam has promised they will go together.

He had written an article about her experiences as a survivor, of her mother's crime and Maidan, of being a bisexual feminist woman in the former USSR, and she has been asked to speak as a special guest on a panel at an American university in October. Slava strengthens her English, has taken a job with a non-profit serving refugees. She writes to her father in Russian. In her mind, she talks to Misha in Ukrainian, and hopes he can hear her.

Velykyy brat, she says, *ya skoro budu vdoma.*

I will be home soon.

Today, Adam and Alexis have brought Slava to their mother's home. Their father is out playing golf. Slava studies the green hills. She still staggers from it. The enormous wealth. The opulent sun. Violet tanning beds and brilliant blue swimming pools. Everything illuminated, neon. Slava, when she is alone, watches the sun set over the sea.

Their mother's front door is made of glass, and as the woman walks up to turn the latch, she looks younger than she is. Hair pulled back, white-blond from both age and salon. Large eyes. The woman moves in a way that Slava can only describe as elegant. When she opens the door, the woman squeezes Slava's hand.

"It's so good to meet you," she says in Russian. "My children have told me about you."

She invites them all in, and Alexis, dressed in jeans with intentional tears, motions for Slava to sit next to her on the couch. Their mother asks if they'd like anything to drink, and when Slava asks for tea, she brings her a glass of iced green.

"Adam says you are from Odesa?" The woman sits across from Slava, next to her son, both of them in mid century modern chairs, holding glasses.

"Yes," Slava says. "But I lived in Kyiv. I left after the protests ended."

The mother asks, "You were at Maidan?"

"Yes," she says. And it also feels impossible that she was.

"My brother," the mother says, her voice becoming weak. "He died at the protests."

Adam leans toward her to hold her hand. The woman is shaking but does not cry. With her other hand, the woman fidgets with a silver ring on a silver chain around her neck.

"Mama thought he passed long ago," Alexis explains. "But a woman called. An American doctor in Ukraine. She asked what to do with his remains. We didn't know what to say. We haven't been sure where to take his ashes—which arrangements to make. Initially, we thought we would take him to Moscow, where they were children. But I met the doctor in Kyiv, before Adam and I picked you up in Odesa, and she gave me a tape. It changed everything."

Slava looks around the room, at the black-and-white photographs on the walls. Photos of Alexis and Adam as children. Photos of their mother's marriage. A framed clipping from a Russian newspaper that read, *BOLSHOI BALLET PERFORMS IN NYC*, and there she is, a young and doe-eyed Anna Ivanova, veiled in shadow, her face upturned toward the light.

BOSTON, UNITED STATES
JUNE 2014

It's in her mother's house that Katya rediscovers the Soviet pin from Aleksandr Ivanovich in her white coat.

She has moved her things into her parents' basement—all in boxes. Her whole life in boxes. Her whole life packed and unpacked. She cuts open the boxes, slicing along the tape.

She lies on her bed, feeling tired, feeling sick. She tells herself it must be the move—must be the ache. Ezra helped her unload the last box when she felt herself about to vomit.

Are you okay, Katya? he asks her, through the door. She opens it. She hugs him goodbye.

When he's gone, she finds her mother in the kitchen. Katya notices her aging. She notices how carefully she cuts the carrots, makes the stew. She kisses Katya and she sings, soft:

Koshenya—Katya Kitten. I love you.

Katya leans her head on her mother's shoulder and asks her, "Did you ever want your own child? Did you ever want to have one on your own?"

Her mother shakes her head at her and says, "You are my child. You are the answer to a prayer."

Before Misha drove Katya back to Kyiv, Misha's mother made her bread to take with her on the drive. She made her a small jar of jam. When Katya said goodbye, Misha's mother replied: *Take this to your mother. It will remind her of home.*

Now, Katya buries herself in the smell of her mother's clothes. She tells her mother, *It's good to be home.*

Katya, in her bathroom mirror, studies herself. She pulls her hair back and examines her face. She thinks of her mothers—both of whom made her. She thinks of Misha's mother. She thinks of the country she came from and the country she was raised into—both feel a dream, and for a moment she isn't sure where she is. She's been her whole life, lost.

She thinks of Misha. She thinks of him and she hesitates, she cries. And the knowledge of what she will never say to him hits her like a swell, like a wave, and she puts her hand below her stomach. She thinks of Isaac and his damaged heart. She breathes.

When she received the call from Misha's mother, she thanked her, and hid her sobs from the receiver. Then Katya told her the only secret she had left.

I would like to name the child after you, Katya said to her.

On the other line, she could hear the old woman cry.

Katya goes to her boy's grave. She kisses the wet grass and leaves a truck on the gravestone. She places flowers for Misha Tkachenko, whose grave she will not be able to visit. His child is growing inside her. Soon, she will feel a kick.

They said it was dead, this land.

You will see, she had said, *how beautiful the garden is.*

ЕПІЛОГ
EPILOGUE

A UKRAINIAN FOLK SONG

Dear Mother, don't cry—I'll return in the spring
as a bird that flies onto your window pane.

I will arrive in the garden with the morning dew,
Or, like the rain, I'll fall at your doorstep.

DANCE OF THE EARTH

Misha sleeps, the afternoon heat causing his shirt to plaster to his chest, his back. Everything is white from the sunlight. She watches him breathing. She looks out the window to the sea. When he wakes, he opens one eye and reaches for her. He finds her belly and kisses her below the navel, her skin hot, her skin taut. She is full of life.

Our daughter will know, she says as they walk. We will take her to where we first met. When she's old enough to know. When she understands the weight of it all.

They walk to the shore together, and the water is blue and warm. The high sun sinking, they go out into the water, then farther, the sand slipping beneath them until they are floating in the sea. Light, like foam.

AFTERWORD

In this year of 2021, it has been nearly eight years since the protests began at Maidan Nezalezhnosti and seven years since the start of the War in Donbass. May this book be a worthy testament for the people of Ukraine.

ACKNOWLEDGEMENTS

This book would not exist in its final form if it had not been for Eric and Eliza—thank you for your tireless dedication, and for caring about this manuscript as deeply as I do. I could not have been more fortunate to end up in such brilliant, dedicated, and skillful hands. Thank you.

My family: Mom, Dad, Jenna, Jon, Dan, Grampa, Nana, Danny. Steph and Katie, thank you for being my sisters. Bethany, you can do anything in this life. I love you.

My best friends Keith and Yaz. Christy and Siz. You are my family forever.

Jenny and Brad—there are not enough words for how much your love and friendship mean to me, how much it has saved me. I would not be *here* without you.

My loves: Corie, Christy and Molly—you have given me the incredible gift of allowing me to feel that I belong, that I am safe and heard, that wins are meant to be celebrated. I love you without measure. Thank you also to Madelynn and Jackie, the alpha and omega of Finer Things, for your kindness, warmth, and laughter. I am grateful to call all of you my friends.

Nikki Jaconelli and Rosalynn Voaden, who cleared the path.

Laura Jesmer and Michael Stoddard, who lit the way.

The Virginia G. Piper Center for Creative Writing for the financial support to travel to Kyiv and Prague in the early stages of this manuscript. Thank you especially to Tito and Angie, who I cannot thank here adequately enough for your compassion when it was most needed.

The Melikian Center and the Critical Languages Institute and their affiliates, especially Keith Brown, Irina Levin, Ana Olenina, Heidi Lenihan and Pani. Deepest gratitude to Narmina Stishehets and Dr. Mark Von Hagen, may he rest in peace.

Finally, thank you to Leah, Beth, Annie, Warren. Chelsea, Joel, Marco. My best and lasting memories are those I spent writing alongside each of you.

Author photograph: Sydney Cisco

Kalani Pickhart holds an MFA in Creative Writing from Arizona State University. She is the recipient of research fellowships from the Virginia G. Piper Center and the U.S. Department of State Bureau of Intelligence for Eastern European and Eurasian Studies. *I Will Die in a Foreign Land* is her first novel.

Books to read!

TRIANGULUM NOVEL BY MASANDE NTSHANGA

⇢ **2020 Nomo Awards Shortlist**
⇢ **A Best Book of 2019** —*LitReactor, Entropy*

⬅ "Magnificently disorienting and meticulously constructed."
—Tobias Carroll, Tor.com

AN AMBITIOUS, OFTEN PHILOSOPHICAL AND GENRE-BENDING NOVEL that covers a period of over 40 years in South Africa's recent past and near future.

A HISTORY OF MY BRIEF BODY
ESSAYS BY BILLY-RAY BELCOURT

⇢ **2021 Lambda Literary Award for Gay Memoir/Biography, Finalist.**
⇢ **"A Best Book of 2020"** —*Kirkus Reviews, Book Riot, CBC, Globe and Mail*

⬅ "Stunning." —Michelle Hart, O, *The Oprah Magazine*

A BRAVE, RAW, AND FIERCELY INTELLIGENT collection of essays and vignettes on grief, colonial violence, joy, love, and queerness.

ALLIGATOR STORIES BY DIMA ALZAYAT

⇢ **PEN/Robert W. Bingham Award, Finalist.**
⇢ **Swansea University Dylan Thomas Prize 2021, Finalist.**
⇢ **James Tait Black Memorial Prize, Finalist.**
⇢ **Short Story Prize, Longlist.**
⇢ **Arab American Book Awards, Honorable Mention.**

⬅ "The richly detailed short fictions in this debut from a Damascus-born scribe form an intricate, breathtaking mosaic of modern Muslim life."
—Michelle Hart, O, *The Oprah Magazine*

THEY CAN'T KILL US UNTIL THEY KILL US ESSAYS BY HANIF ABDURRAQIB

⇢ **Best Books 2017:** NPR, *Rolling Stone, Buzzfeed, Paste Magazine, Esquire, Chicago Tribune, Vol. 1 Brooklyn, Entropy, Heavy, Book Riot,* among others.

⬅ "A much-needed collection for our time. [Abdurraqib] has proven to be one of the most essential voices of his generation." —Juan Vidal, NPR

⬅ "A collection of death-defying protest songs for the Black Lives Matter era." —Walton Muyumba, *Chicago Tribune*

THE HARE NOVEL BY MELANIE FINN

⬅ "[A] brooding feminist thriller." —*New York Times*
⬅ "Finn has a gift for weaving existential and political concerns through tautly paced prose." —Molly Young, *Vulture*

AN ASTOUNDING NEW LITERARY THRILLER from a celebrated author at the height of her storytelling prowess, *The Hare* bravely considers a woman's inherent sense of obligation—sexual and emotional—to the male hierarchy.

Thank you for supporting independent culture!